To Find
A Killer

Charlie Vogel

To Find A Killer is a work of fiction. Names, characters and incidents are products of the author's imagination or are used fictitiously. Any resemblance to actual events or locales or persons, living or dead, is entirely coincidental.

Published 2002 by
The Fiction Works
Lake Tahoe, Nevada
www.fictionworks.com

ISBN 1-58124-688-9
Printed in the
United States of America

To Find
A Killer

Chapter One

The man in the Sergio Valente suit stumbled but held his balance as he avoided a collision with the right front fender of my sport's car. He stepped over the yellow curb and faded into the waves of employees. The twelve-story office building painted a long shadow, absorbing the throng exiting the glass doors. I assumed the missing man took the responsibility for the near-accident, since he had run in front of me. I had the right of way.

Rubbing the right front wheel against the curb, I parked my new Ferrari Boxer facing the "No Parking" sign. The late afternoon sun reflected brightly off the deep red hood. I turned my head away from the glare and stared out the tinted passenger window, watching the shapely legs of the office girls passing by.

The Bison Insurance building towered above the metropolis. I glanced once more at the glass doors, then turned my attention back to the mini-skirts. My wife should be coming through the employee's exit any moment.

While waiting, I reminisced my college days at Northwestern University, where Eileen had majored in business and I worked on a Bachelor's in Fine Arts. Twenty-five years had passed since we got those degrees. Twenty-five years. We met at a benefit dance. I couldn't remember which organization had sponsored the event. In the mid 60's it could have been a fraternity or some anti-war movement for all we cared!

Right after graduation, we married against her father's wishes. Since she was his only child, he finally acknowledged us, giving her two million in cash as a gift with the stipulation the gift was hers. It didn't matter. In defiance, we decided to make our home near him in Pecatonica, Nebraska, the city her family had "owned" for decades. We packed our few belongings into an old Volkswagen van and pointed the smokey exhaust towards Chicago. Ten hours later, a tow truck dumped the "Love Van" at the front gate of her father's Pecatonica mansion.

She accepted a position at Bison Insurance, a large Nebraska firm, and I took a teaching job at East High School. Over the years, she fared much better financially than I and we still didn't mind. She became an executive in charge of Policy Frauds, while I struggled through year after year of teaching art to uncaring kids.

With her income and despite her father, we purchased a large home at 10286 Pacific. Our neighbors went to work each day to their law offices and medical clinics. They thought as much of my teaching as my father-in-law, so I didn't socialize much. Eileen represented us, mainly at her father's insistence.

Pectonica, a city of four hundred thousand, did not compare to my hometown of Highland Park, Illinois. I had always felt cramped living near Chicago. In Nebraska I could drive ten minutes, be outside the city, and breathe in the foul air of country cows. As a trade off, the Interstate system provided a short drive to the cultured university life in Lincoln, the state capitol.

Except for her father's frequent interference, life had been good for us in this Missouri River town. A month had passed since the May 22, 1993, celebration of my forty-seventh birthday. Eileen had purchased this Ferrari Boxer for my gift. I had to spend only one month of my teacher's salary to insure it.

A shapely blonde hesitated near the door then stepped aside and waved on by my wife. The door opened and the warm breeze instantly filled the car with Eileen's scent,"France's Amour." Her dark hair covered her face as she bent to slide into the seat. Out of habit, I gently touched her lips with mine and murmured, "How was work today?"

While my gaze and mind lingered on the scenery beyond the car window, I heard her rather stiff and routine, "Fine, dear. How was your day?"

Sitting back, I studied her. "What's wrong?"

"Wrong? You mean with my work day? I-I found a discrepancy in one of the Vice President's life insurance policy. It has nagged at me for hours, but I'm sure it will be worked out tomorrow. You know how I hate unresolved problems. Did you call Morris Cadillac to see if my car has been serviced?"

"I forgot. Is it too late to call now?"

"They close in fifteen minutes. What have you done all day? Unlike me, you do have the summer off. I would think you had time to make one phone call."

Directing the car into traffic, I glanced at her frown. Even when she was pissed, she was beautiful. I pressed my foot on the gas pedal so the squeal from the rear tires could add sound effects to the Neil Diamond song rising from the speakers. After clearing a space between two inexpensive foreign cars, I unhooked the phone from the dash and handed it to her. "Here. Give them a call. We can make it in fifteen minutes."

She replaced the phone. "Never mind. Let's stop at your favorite hang-out, that Stop-and-Go near 120th and Dodge. I need a Coke. So, what did you do all day?"

"This morning I had coffee with Ernie . . . the music teacher you can't stand?"

"I like him. It's his wife who's a bitch."

"Anyway . . . this afternoon I signed up for courses at the University."

"More? Oh, I forgot. It's mandatory continuing ed. Right?"

Silence. My hands opened and closed on the steering wheel. I knew what was coming next.

"I wish you would quit teaching and come to work at the insurance company. That great opening in advertising is still there."

"Yeah, but I like my summers off, remember?" My deliberate and too-fast turn into the parking lot squealed the front tires this time. Another twist of the steering wheel and I whipped into a space near the glass doors of the Stop-and-Go. Eileen threw a glare my way as we slammed to a stop.

I quickly combed my lengthy, gray-brown hair straight back and worked a rubber band around the pony tail. Eileen still hadn't moved. The idea of opening the door for her flashed through my mind. It had been years since I had shown her that kind of attention. Since buying tailored suits to match her corporate rise, she had taken on the general air of an independent woman who opened her own doors before I could even tilt the steering wheel. This time she just sat as I got out.

"What's the matter? Aren't you coming in? You're the one who wanted to stop."

She sighed heavily then flipped down the sun visor for a long look in the mirror. "Okay. My mind's just stuck on work. Something's not . . . Let's go in . . ." She frowned then looked from the visor mirror to the side-door mirror.

I peered over the top of the car to see what had caught her attention behind us. An old van sat at the curb across the street.

"What's wrong now? You're acting like you just stepped out of a Stephen King movie."

First she jerked her coin purse from her handbag then shoved the black leather clutch under the seat. "I've got to call work, but from the pay phone inside. Forget my car for now. You will call tomorrow. Right?"

Trying to avoid stepping on her heels, I clenched my teeth. "Yeah, I'm educated, not totally stupid. But, we still have time to make it today."

"Tomorrow, I said. I've got other business right now."

I reached around to hold the glass door open for her. Looking up, I smiled at the familiar face behind the counter. "Hi, Harry! How's it going?"

The middle-aged, slender man stood at the register, habitually turned so customers didn't immediately notice the empty sleeve pinned to his left shoulder. He tossed loose change into the appropriate compartments of the open drawer then smacked it shut with a blur of movement. I learned long ago how not to stare at his facial scars, how to see the man behind the sharp eyes.

"Hi, there, Bob. Who's the pretty young thing with you? Don't say Mrs. Norris."

"Well, yeah, it is the one and only. You finally caught me with my wife."

"No wonder you ain't got a girlfriend. If I had something like her, I'd be permanently attached, too. What can I do for you, guy?"

"While Eileen is using the phone, could you ring up a couple of Cokes? I'll be in the back getting a six-pack of beer."

Eileen slipped coins into the phone as I passed and didn't even look up. She still frowned, deep in troubled thought. I opened the beer cooler. The refrigeration motor kicked on with a loud hum that rattled the metal shelves.

Behind me I heard metal scraping metal, a sound from my high school days when I went hunting with my dad. A shell being pumped into the chamber of a shotgun.

Eileen turned toward me, intent on her instructions to her secretary about a file box. I lost the rest of her words as I focused my hearing on the front of the store. Quiet. Too quiet. Casually, I shifted for a better view down the aisle.

Harry's right arm stretched before him, palm up as if halting someone. Almost in slow motion he lowered the hand and began to punch register keys.

A tall, thick-bodied man stepped to the counter, his back to me. He indeed held the butt of a shotgun against his armpit. Cold fear swept over me, tightening my chest and my knees at the same time. I thought about trying for the rear storage room exit, but when I turned I faced another, slighter man. A black scarf hid a face shadowed by a red baseball cap. His dark eyes stared directly into mine. I glanced down at the handgun in his right hand. He held it steady.

Remembering details had always been my special talent, probably due to my ability to draw and paint. Fear melted into curiosity as I collected his details. Why is a robber wearing expensive designer jeans and Giorgio Italian shoes?

"What the hell is going on?" Eileen demanded behind me.

As I turned to her voice, so did the man with the shotgun. "Everyone, freeze! Mister, you drop your wallet on the floor. And you, Lady, you drop your purse."

As Eileen threw her coin purse to the floor, I eased my hand toward my back pocket. The man behind me beat me to it, first clumsily pulling my wallet free then smacking me between the shoulder blades with that gun. I lost my balance and sprawled forward.

Eileen's low-heeled shoes moved just a few feet from my face. A shot exploded like a single firecracker, concussing off the glass cooler. The missile zinged above me and I automatically pressed myself into the tile floor. I looked up just as Eileen crumpled near me. My insides clenched, expecting the slam of a bullet. Yet, my eyes remained focus on Eileen's mussed hair. She didn't move. Had she been shot? Why would she be shot and not me?

I listened hard before glancing around. The nearby gunman was gone. Slowly I inched towards my wife. "Eileen!" I whispered loudly. "Honey? Are you all right?" Voices sounded behind me, but I didn't care what they said. I had to get to Eileen.

Then I was close enough to touch her face. Her big, beautiful eyes stared, just stared back at me. "Eileen! Goddamn it! Say something!"

A hand settled on my shoulder. I looked up into Harry's scarred face. The sadness there forced me to shout, "Get me some help! I don't think she's breathing!"

CPR flashed through my mind. Yes, I know CPR. I turned her onto her back. My fingers tugged at the silken loop of her blouse tie. I frantically ripped buttons free. Cradling her head in one hand, I swept my shaking fingers through her mouth. Then I settled my mouth around her lips and blew once, twice. Water bubbled in her throat. I turned to see her chest move. It didn't. Everything was smeared with red, her clothes, my hands, the floor, Harry's fingers pressed into the side of Eileen's throat. I looked up into his tear-filled eyes. He swung his head from side-to-side, his expression reflecting my agony.

He understood like no one else. He had served in Vietnam as a medic and lost his arm in a mine explosion. I had dodged the draft by keeping high grades and not getting my number picked. The closest I had come to death was crying over the Kent State students. Now the experienced Harry pulled me against him and we cried over Eileen's dead body.

The paramedics arrived, pushing me aside. For hour-long minutes I watched as they traded places with police officers then the coroner's stretcher. Toneless words responded to hollow questions. Finally, a Sergeant Morten led me to the store's dirty break room.

Harry shoved me down into a chair then placed a cup of coffee in my hand. I looked up into Morten's stare and blinked at the hardness I found. Suddenly his attitude registered. He thought I was lying about something.

"Tell me again, Mr. Norris. What did the suspect have on?"

"Why do you keep asking? I told you the same thing a half dozen times."

"I can't understand why you can give me a detailed description on one person, but you can't remember if the guy with the shotgun had a blue or red scarf over his face."

"Like I said, he had his back to me most of the time. Didn't Harry here give you a description?"

"Yeah, but I want to hear it from you."

"I've told you everything."

"Sure. Well, I'll be at the station to finish my reports. Thanks for your help, Mr. Norris." He stood, slurping down the last of his coffee.

"Wait a minute!" I raised my voice. "What about my wife?"

"I am terribly sorry about your loss, Mr. Norris. When we catch the robbery suspects, we'll let you know."

"No, wait. You keep referring to these men as robbery suspects. What about the one who killed my wife? Wouldn't he be charged with murder?"

"Yeah, but we have to clear up the robbery first since that was the primary crime. Look, Mr. Norris, we have had identical robberies about once every two weeks in this area. I have to admit this is the first shooting and the first time there's been more than one man, but the shotgun, the masks, the baseball caps, the timing has all been the same.

"So what have you been doing about them, for God's sake?"

Morten drew himself up, obviously angry about being challenged. "We call witnesses, talk to ex-cons and snitches . . . Why are you asking? Think we're not doing our job?"

"Apparently you haven't been." My voice shook with my contempt. "Otherwise these lowlifes would have been apprehended by now . . . and my wife would still be alive."

"You, Buddy, have no idea of the work we do to arrest a suspect—"

"I don't give a damn how much work you have to do. I want that asshole who killed my wife. If you don't find him, I will go out onto those streets and find him myself! Do you understand?"

"Do whatever you want, but let me warn you. If you ain't street-wise, you ain't gonna find shit on any street . . . Do you under-stand?"

The plain clothes detective shouldered Harry out of the way then stomped down the aisle to the glass doors. His hand smacked them open, sliding across the finger-print dust left by the lab technicians.

My fingers pressed into the styrofoam cup as if leaving prints of my own. So he doesn't think I can do it. I had always thought of myself as intelligent, resourceful, and willing to take risks . . . when there was a reason. Now, I had a reason. If the cops couldn't find this guy, I would. I'd even buy a gun of my own, if necessary.

"Bob?" Harry's voice intruded.

"Yeah? I-I was thinking."

"Saw that, but I gotta lock up. I ain't got enough cash to stay open. The district manager won't be here for a couple of hours."

Settling into the Ferrari, I inhaled the perfume that I knew would always linger in the car. The drive home passed in a blur as I tried to ignore the empty seat beside me.

Steering into our driveway, I pressed the garage door opener twice. Nothing happened. I turned off the engine and irritably marched to the front door I hadn't entered in over a year. My fingers fumbled for the unfamiliar key then I remembered the extra key hidden under the nearby concrete flower pot. As I bent to retrieve that key, I saw the door was already open.

Cautious yet stunned, I moved from one ransacked room to another. Pictures had been taken from the walls, cushions ripped open, glassware swept from shelves to shatter on the floor, draw-ers emptied, books and papers strewn everywhere. I finally found the living room phone under a pile of dirt dumped from a potted plant. The repetitious questions of the 911 operator annoyed me as much as Sergeant Morten's. A moment later I called my brother in Chicago to report the day's horror. The thought of calling my father-in-law never entered my mind.

Chapter Two

The crowd slowly fanned out from the grave, some people form-
ing into small groups, others searching for their cars. My gaze
roamed over friends and family. Some names just wouldn't come to
me. It didn't matter, not really. I turned back to the casket. It rested
above the grave. She must be lonely. Eileen had never been lonely.
Someone had always been at her side.

Standing next to me, my father-in-law accepted a clean handkerchief from his chauffeur. I had not stood this close to the man in
over two years. I couldn't help staring at the reserved business
tycoon as he dried tears from his swollen eyes. To my imagination
he looked like someone had pasted rusted wool pads atop his
coconut-shaped head, then carefully wrapped his bony body in a
DaVinci suit.

Why did I dislike this man? Did it start when he didn't want
Eileen to marry me? Or five years later when he sneered his hatred
for my middle-class family? He actually hired a security agency to
pry into my background when I wouldn't satisfy his demanding
questions. He found my past dull, uneventful, ordinary. The fact
that my relatives shopped at discount stores and bought clothes off
the rack must have really insulted . . .

I forced my attention back to the present and his grief-filled eyes.
I had held back my own tears for most of the ceremony, determined
to nurture my pain my own way. However, my choked words gave
more than I wanted to him. "Henry, I will never forgive myself for
letting her die."

His mouth moved as he tried to form a suitable sentence. He
turned to his chauffeur, almost as if reaching for some support.
Then his back stiffened and he swung back, his face controlled.
"Robert, she had been my little girl for forty years. I have lost
everything precious to me. Money will not bring her back. I know
that. But, at least I can make your future miserable here in
Pecatonica."

"What are you getting at?"

"Why-why did you take her to a-a convenience store? And, of all places, in a lower class neighborhood?"

Heat rose into my face. An involuntary surge of tears slipped down my cheeks. "Damn you, Henry! I did not kill her. You can't blame the shooting itself on me! Whatever you do with your god-damn money, you will never make me more miserable than I am right now!"

"Robert, calm . . . down. I didn't say you killed her. But you can't deny you placed her outside her environment, in a store more suit-ed to-to people like . . . servants." He trembled with the effort to control himself.

Servants, huh? People like me? A barely tolerated Robert. He couldn't call me Bob, like everyone else did. Bob. A simple name, spelled the same forward and backward. No, here he stands forcing himself to be polite, even when he's being an asshole.

"Henry, I don't know exactly what happened, but you can bank on this . . . I'm going to find out the reason she died."

My father-in-law's pointed chin rose. "Charles, please bring my car around."

Chucky stepped away in military fashion before Henry deigned to speak to me again. "Although it may be uncomfortable for both of us, I do hope we see each other more often. Why? For the sake of Eileen's . . . memory. It is sad that it took the death . . . of my daughter to bring us here, to stand side by side and . . . converse even this limited amount. The last time was when you arrived at my door twenty some years ago, I believe.

"I remember at my beloved Veronica's funeral that I first met her aunt, a woman born into the family out of wedlock. Now, we get together at least twice a year. Maybe funerals are meant to bring the living closer together. Do you think so, Robert?"

I barely heard him. My mind began working on a startling observation. Eileen had not looked anything like her mother or this man before me. Actually, her features had resembled . . . Chucky's.

"Robert?"

"I . . . guess you could say that. If you don't mind, would you leave me with Eileen for a few minutes?"

"Of course. We can talk later at the luncheon. Speaking of which, why did you decide to have it in a church basement? My home would have been more adequate."

I only shrugged in reply. He cocked an indignant eyebrow at my rudeness then walked stiffly toward his limousine, alone. I waited until the door closed on him before sitting on one of the grave side chairs. The flower-strewn casket filled my senses. Eileen had always liked plenty of room, whether it was in her large cars or our spacious home. Now, she had been shoved into a small box, an expensive shell, a confined space she probably hated.

A gentle hand on my shoulder brought me to my feet. My brother Donald led me away. As I walked I felt like I had forgotten something. I had to go back and tell Eileen something. My blurred vision forced me to lower my chin onto my chest. I didn't want anybody to see me cry.

Donald opened the door to his family station wagon. His wife and two teenaged daughters had left with an aunt from who knew where. Everyone was to meet at the church for all that family exchange of feelings and memories. I asked Donald to take me home.

I walked pass the Ferrari, still in front of the closed garage doors. I hadn't called about Eileen's Cadillac. As I unlocked the front door, I thought of selling it and the Ferrari, too, simply because I never wanted to drive either car again. Why not sell everything, the furniture, the house, anything that reminded me of Eileen? I dropped into a living room chair, my head tilted back as I pondered that cloudy future.

A few minutes later, Donald placed a steaming "Old Fart" mug of coffee on the glass table before me. I stared a moment. Eileen would never allow anyone to drink or eat over the white furniture and carpet in that room.

Carefully I picked up the mug and rose with "Let's go out on the patio."

He nodded his bald head, being just as careful with his mug. One finger nervously toyed with his mustache. "I'll be right there after I make a phone call."

"Don't spill anything on the carpet and tell Bonnie to put a double fudge brownie in a doggy bag for me."

"Will do," he replied with a grunt.

The sliding glass doors opened soundlessly. I walked across the flagstones, my heels clicking too loudly. A discarded towel, rained on twice in the past week, allowed me to wipe dust from a lounge chair. I savored Donald's coffee then leaned back. My older brother always seemed to know how to be the friend I needed, not too nosy, not too judgmental, just there. He stayed in Chicago after college and even raised a family in the same house we had grown up in.

By the time I drained my mug, Donald had joined me. Immediately he removed his dark jacket and loosened his tie. His gaze swept the tiled pool and landscaped grounds as he lit up a cigarette. "Want one?"

"Nope."

"More coffee?"

"Nope."

Finally, he sat down and studied me. "So . . . how's teaching?"

"About as boring as sitting in an office selling imports from China."

"Well, little brother, my import business brings in a good income. It helped you get through school and it's going to get my kids through college, too. I'm not tired of it, but you sound tired."

"Yup. I'm calling the school tomorrow and quitting."

"Bullshit! You can't give up your career!"

"Why? I'm financially set. I don't owe money on one damn thing. I'll sell all this and get a smaller place. I'll even get a car like one of yours, only not as big. Maybe something like an Escort."

"Oh, right. Why do you want to give up teaching?"

"You said it. I'm tired of teaching art. It takes up too much time. I . . . I want to be creative, to produce something of my own. I want to return to painting. Yeah, painting. Kids don't appreciate the feeling of creativity. They take the class thinking it's an easy course and they need the credits. But . . . most important, Eileen wanted me to quit teaching."

"Ah." He drew on his cigarette, concentrating on the exhaled smoke. "For what it's worth, I think you are going through a phase of adjustment. With Eileen gone, you're giving up. You need a little rest. Get away to a cabin. Do some fishing. But don't—" He stubbed out his cigarette on the bottom of his shoe. "Give up your career and your home. You spent a lot of time and money on what you have here."

"What money? I didn't spend one dime for any of this. It's all Eileen's. And what the hell is time? Time isn't something I value. Time is such an abstraction in life." I leaned forward, my elbows on my knees, my hands clenched. "Look . . . How can I explain this? Eileen was all I had. Now that she's gone, I have only one thing, one purpose. I will have the man who killed her." I clenched my jaw. "Since time has no importance, I can hunt for him quietly."

"You-You're talking nonsense. Let the police handle this. They don't need you butting in. Dammit, I don't want you meddling. I remember that time in high school you didn't think the principal cared who stole your coat. You shot off your mouth at the school board meeting and almost got the man fired!"

"He deserved it. I never got my goddamn coat back, did I? But you know this is different, Donald. This was Eileen's life. It deserves to be avenged. There has to be a way to find this murderer. This city isn't half the size of Chicago. If I roam around down by the tracks, I might find something. I know there's a lot of criminals types living around the downtown area and the railroad—"

Donald held up a hand. "Wait a minute! How do you know where the crooks live? Have you ever been in that section of town?"

"I've driven through there several times in twenty-five years of living here. I've seen the shoddy bars and hotels. I'm sure that's where the scum would hang out."

"Bob, listen! Stay out of places you don't belong! Do you hear me?"

"I hear you, brother, but I'm not listening! I've made up my mind. I will live like scum . . . if that's what it takes. I will search every crack in this city until I find the killer. No one . . . not you . . . not my illustrious father-in-law . . . not the police . . . will stop me. I've thought it out. In the morning I'm going to visit Harry at the Stop-and-Go. He gets a lot of characters in his store. I have a feeling he can point me in the right direction."

"You mean the wrong direction. Wait, before you say anything more . . . how are you going to handle the estate you will leave behind?"

"You have that little faith in me, huh? Well, smart ass, another call I'm making tomorrow is to my attorney so I can put you in charge of everything. You will sell it all, pay whatever bills come and bank the remainder in an interest-baring checking account. I'll live off that interest. Low-rent housing, a few crumby clothes, my paints and canvas, an occasional meal . . . I'll survive nicely . . . until I find the bastard."

We stared into one another's eyes until determination overcame reluctance. Donald shook his head and stood with his hand extended. I clasped it warmly. It felt good. "You do that, Bob. Yes, sir. You do that. I have to pick up Bonnie and the kids. That four hundred and fifty mile drive home will be a long one."

"Today? You're driving to Chicago right away?"

"We'll probably stop in Des Moines for the night. What's the problem?"

"But we have work to do. I thought you would stay long enough to get things started tomorrow."

"Well, you thought wrong. Maybe you can react spontaneously, little brother, but I have a business to run. I'm not doing all your goddamn work while you lay around a shit hole and play cop. You forgot how the family calls me 'the responsible one.' As soon as you get your affairs ready, have your attorney call me. I'll oversee the damn bank account so you don't starve . . . but that's all I'm going to do for you."

Chapter Three

The piercing ring of the phone bounced around the dead cells of my brain. I knew I had screwed up when I switched to Scotch after drinking only beer for several hours. Reaching over the sheet covering my face, I felt for the curved plastic of the receiver and finally found it near the end of the sofa. The cotton shield slid away and the blinding sun hit my burning eyes. "Hello!" I loudly cleared my scratchy throat.

"Mr. Norris?"

"Yeah, you found me."

"This is Maggie Holmes at Bison Insurance. Your late wife's secretary?"

The memory neurons slowly clicked into place. I coughed and attempted some dignity. "Oh, yes, Maggie. You were at the funeral. I-I'm sorry I didn't get a chance to talk to you. I was sort of . . . preoccupied."

"Yes, Mr. Norris, I understand. But there is something important I have to tell you. Very important. May we meet for lunch today? Or tomorrow . . . at the latest."

I tried to think through the items on my own all-important agenda. "What time is it anyway?"

"Oh! Oh, I must have awakened you. I'm so sorry. It's nine o'clock."

Sitting up with the sheet bunched across my lap, I felt a chunk of acid bile traveling up my throat. Hm, the Italian sausage I washed down with the Scotch? The image of lunch made me swallow several times without success. "How about dinner? Tonight at seven. Carlo's. No! I-I had Italian last night." The sausage spiraled up further. "Any quick suggestion?"

"How about seven at Merrill's? They have steaks. I could make reservations—"

"Great. Thanks. Tonight." I fumbled the receiver and dashed for the bathroom.

Several long minutes later, I sucked a piece of strawberry hard candy to camouflage the taste of reprocessed stomach contents. The cold, wet cloth I held to my forehead helped my headache just enough for me to think.

With a couple of ice cubes nestled in the washcloth, I spent the next hour on the phone with Winters, my attorney. Henry paid the man a monthly salary. Assumed the man still represented the entire family, I didn't mention a bill. Anyway, he never brought up payment for his services. In fact, his voice sounded almost bored with my list of directives. Papers rustled in the background just before he crisply informed me a well-qualified financial advisor and a reputable real estate company would be notified. Of course, I would have legal papers to sign before finalizing any transactions. His office could notify me or I would have to call from time to time. His lack of enthusiasm made me think of Henry. I told him I would be in touch on a regular basis and enjoyed slamming the phone in his arrogant ear.

The casual old jeans felt comfortable, but not as right as the "Grateful Dead" T-shirt I slipped on. My gaze settled on the box in the bottom of the closet containing the Nike's Eileen had hated, so I had never worn. I jerked the shoes on, deciding a run would clear my head. Exercise was good for a hang-over, at least for any hangover I ever had. And I had to get my thoughts in order, to gain perspective and plan.

Jogging in the direction of Harry's distant Stop-and-Go, I realized it had been a year or more since I last ran. Within one block, stiff leg muscles protested. Once upon a time six miles had been nothing. Now, two miles looked questionable. I should have called to see if Harry was even at the store. But he always seems to be there. There? I almost stumbled. Why was I going back to where Eileen died? To make myself suffer? No, I have to talk to Harry. Something about Harry is important.

I passed Judge Jerry Williams working in his lawn. Everyone in the neighborhood hired a lawn service, except a guy who could most afford it. Retired from the bench for ten years, he still enjoyed landscape gardening in that yard.

Out of breath, I stopped. Sausage and booze mingled in my involuntary belch. Maybe the old guy wouldn't notice. "Hi, Jerry! How's it going?"

Williams looked up then shifted and awkwardly rose from his knees. A piece of sod dropped from one wrinkled hand as he cocked his head to look at me. His eyes squinted then adjusted behind his thick trifocals. A smile of recognition parted his sun-dried lips. "Well, Bob! How are you doing? Ah, you look a little pale."

"I'm fine. Everything's fine. I'm just not . . . used to jogging. Thought I'd start up again."

"That's nice. A young man like you should be in good shape. Can't wallow in sorrow . . . I mean, I am sorry about your wife. Wished I had met her before . . . Ah, she did look beautiful at the funeral. Of course, they always do . . . Bob, are you sure you aren't getting sick? Maybe it's the sun. Would you like a glass of water?"

"Yeah. Thanks, Jerry. I think I'll take you up on the offer."

"Come on up to the patio. It's shady and much cooler. The sun gets to me too, you know."

I leaned back into his ornate metal lawn chair, eyes closed, trying to control my body and my thoughts. The old man returned with two tall glasses of lemonade. He settled in a chair across the table, studying me with a smile. "You put away a lot of snake bite last night, eh?"

The lemonade went down wrong. I coughed. "How did you guess?"

"Did the same thing when my wife died a few years back. I spent three days drowning myself in the bottom of cheap wine bottles. I can smell it sweating out of you. There's something in that glass that should make you feel better."

"Lemonade?"

"And a little gin. Not enough to make things worse, just enough to relax . . . ah, those shaky muscles of yours. We used to add a little gin to the punch when I was young, just enough to relax the girls or, rather, weaken their resistance."

"Yeah," I nodded with an understanding smile of my own, "I can see how that would help." A large gulp of the biting sweetness slid down easily. The soothing effects settled in my stomach and soon radiated into my body. By the end of the lemonade, I was feeling much better. I didn't notice the pitcher on the table until the judge refilled my glass.

"Thanks, Jerry, but this has to be my last. I-I didn't stop by to commiserate . . . exactly. I want to sort of ask a favor."

"What do you need?"

"Do you still have those emergency keys to my house?"

"Yes. Do you want them back?"

"No-No. On that ring is an extra key for the Ferrari. It's been parked in my drive since . . . Would you mind putting it in the garage and kind of keeping an eye on the house for me?"

"No problem." He settled back in his chair, frowning, his fingers tapping his glass. "Are you leaving?"

"For a bit, but I will keep in touch, ah, call you to check on things. Which reminds me. Can I use your phone?"

"Sure." He pulled a cordless phone from inside his unfashionable bib overalls.

I dialed the Stop-and-Go, hoping to hear a familiar voice.

I wasn't disappointed. "Hi, Harry. This is Bob Norris. If you're going to be there for a bit, I need to talk to you."

"You caught me on my way out the door. I'm starting at a different place. I-I can't work here. You know. I kinda hurt every time I even look at the spot where your wife . . . Well, I got transferred to a store closer to my apartment."

"Great, but . . . Harry, I really need to talk to you. Can I meet you somewhere . . . right now, if you have time?"

"Well, there's the Burger Place at 108th and Dodge. Guess that's not far from your house."

I thought about my muscles, now relaxed from the judge's therapy. "I'll be there in twenty minutes."

That second glass went down even smoother than the first. I knew for sure I would be able to make 108th and Dodge without pain. Probably run back, too. Maybe run a circle around the entire city. My renewed strength lasted until my face almost met the sidewalk a block from the burger joint.

I carefully rolled onto my back, took deep breaths, and wiped the sweat from my eyes with the bottom of my "Dead" T-shirt. High above me, the clouds slowly spun clockwise. Then the lemonade geysered from my mouth and flowed over my chin and neck. Eyes pinched closed, I awaited death.

A voice echoed from the distance. "Bob? What the hell's the matter with you?"

One of my uncoordinated hands again wiped my face with the T-shirt. I managed to cautiously turn on my side, eyes open. One cough and I felt able to speak, sounding brighter than I felt. "Harry! What brings you here?"

His arm snaked under my arm pit and pulled me upright. Damn, he's strong. Wouldn't want to piss him off. Shakily, I stood on my own two feet. He looked me up and down, his nose wrinkling.

"I was driving by when I saw you stumbled. Couldn't tell if you were tired or drunk . . . until I got here. Better keep walking or your legs are going to cramp."

"Sure. Yeah. I remember now. I was on my way to meet you. Jogging. Guess I'm not in good enough shape. I probably should have warmed up. Yeah. Warmed up."

He shook his head, his hand clutching my T-shirt to keep me steady and moving. "What you needed was wheels. Why the hell did you decide to jog all that way?"

"Well, after I got done barfing the first time this morning, I looked in the mirror. Here was this beer gut. Didn't matter if I died doing six miles or even two miles, but I had to get rid of this flab."

"Man, you are not in your twenties! At your age you expected to pound out six miles without working up to it? Get in the car. I'll drive you home and get a bowl of soup down you. You haven't eaten, have you?"

"Neighbor gave me some fruit juice," I tried to sound funny. Didn't seem to work.

Harry merely shoved me into the passenger seat of his 1979 Honda. I started to close my eyes but they scraped open when he attempted to slam the door shut, again and again. Finally, he grabbed a length of clothes line from the backseat, kneed the door closed, and wrapped the line around the open-windowed door frame and the center pillar. It was rather interesting how he managed to tie it off with that one hand and his teeth. At least the driver's door stayed shut after he climbed in. A series of whining noises came from the engine as he attempted to start it.

"Problems?" I tried to sound conversational since funny hadn't worked.

He didn't bother looking at me. "The fly wheel has notches in the teeth. Sooner or later it'll catch."

"Glad you don't have to rush me to the hospital. Why don't you get a better car? This rust bucket has about had it!"

That made him look at me, but his eyes didn't seem especially friendly. "'Cause I ain't got the money. At the end of the month, I have just enough for rent and food."

"Rent, huh. Where do you live?"

The engine roared to life. "Missouri View apartments. It's in the luxury district, down by the tracks on 7th and Jackson."

"It's a nice place?"

Harry's stomach pressed against the steering wheel to hold it steady as he engaged the floor gear shift. We moved into the flow of traffic. His belly held the wheel as he shifted up again. A deep horn sounded. I turned my head and saw "Peterbilt" spread across the rear window. Harry concentrated on what was in front of him, ignoring the truck's huge chrome grill that had to fill his rearview mirror. I pressed down in my seat.

"Nice place?" He mimicked me. "It's a one room with a fold-out bed and plenty of cockroaches to keep me company. 'Course, the bugs ain't as bad as the rats. I killed two of those by my refrigerator just last week."

I felt a little motion sick as the Honda sped up and slowed down with the traffic. Harry whipped around a corner on two wheels, leaving behind the truck's blaring horn.

"Would you mind taking me to your place, instead of mine? If you stop somewhere, I can buy that can of soup."

The Honda slowed. "Why would you want to go to my home? Like I just said, it's a dump and dirty. I don't clean much."

"I don't want to stay at my house. I'm selling everything I own. Period. I want to move into an apartment."

Harry guided the car into a parking lot and pulled into an empty space. He turned to stare at me. I saw wariness and sympathy in his expression. "That's why you wanted to meet with me?" He shook his head. "Listen, Bob. I don't know what you're thinking so soon after . . . but you don't want to move into my pad or one like it! I pay one hundred and fifty bucks a month for a view of the tracks with rats, fleas, and cockroaches as roomies. You'd find it kinda crowded."

I studied a Ford dealership sign at the end of the block. The vague thoughts I hadn't been able to pin down about Harry and his way of life settled into place. I straightened in the seat. "Not necessarily your apartment, then. I'll find one close to you."

"Bob! You ain't listening!" He began speaking like I was a simpleton or too drunk to hear. "The apartments on my end of town are all the same. You don't want to live in the slums. Look west. You can afford those new places going up all over. You'll be happier."

"Drive to that corner and turn right."

"But this street doesn't lead anywhere!"

"Turn into that car lot. I want to find a vehicle."

The frowning Harry did as directed then followed me as I roamed from new cars to used cars and back. He even held the glass door for me so I could enter the showroom in search of a salesman.

A tall, slick-dressed man blocked my path. He assessed me, a false smile pasted in place. "May I help you?"

I glanced down at my vomit-stained shirt and worn jeans. Over my shoulder, I saw Harry had returned to his Honda. He leaned against the fender, his expression still dark. I hooked my thumbs in my front pockets mimicking Harry's stance, only I didn't frown at the salesman. I challenged him. "I want to buy a car."

"And what type of car do you wish?"

"Something that runs, without floor vents like that Honda out there."

"Ah, what do you mean?"

"Well, every time we hit a bump, the vents get bigger and the view of the road broader. Pretty soon, I'll be able to stop by dragging my feet. I don't want that."

His patience came to an end. His tone changed from nice to annoyed. "We have a few out back that will probably suit you. What can you pay?"

I leaned my head forward, looking down at my fingers drumming on my hips. Narrowing my eyes, I looked up with "I want something like that." My thumb pointed into the showroom.

"Right. That's a Mustang. This year's model. It's probably out of your price range."

"I'll pay cash."

He snickered, yellow cigarette stains showing on his teeth. "I'm sure you will. I'm busy, mister. Look around all you want. If you see anything in that back lot you want, write down the number on the windshield and come back here. I'll see what can be worked out."

I walked around him and eyed the sticker in the Mustang's rear window. With exaggerated care, I pulled my checkbook from my rear pocket, entered the list price, scribbled my signature, and handed him the check, along with my driver's license. My eyebrow arched as the salesman looked from the check to the photo on the license to my face. I smiled wickedly with a tight "Call the bank . . . now!"

After he disappeared into a cubicle office at the back, I pointedly ignored my appearance and slid behind the wheel of the sports car. I examined the panel gauges and n niceties then squirmed in the seat. Yeah, this will work.

The salesman reappeared with a genuine grin on his lips, a stunned glaze to his eyes. His mouth moved but nothing came out.

"Everything all right?" I couldn't help the smugness.

"Y-yes. Fine, just fine. I'm . . . I'm terribly sorry, sir. I obviously made a big mistake. First impressions and all that . . . Ah, I mean, you just take your time. Look at any car you wish. Of course, I'll be right at your side to answer any questions."

"How much of a trade will you give me on my friend's Honda?"

"It's . . . oh, probably worth a couple hundred."

"Give me two thousand for it and you can keep the sticker price check for the Mustang."

"But, Mr. Norris, that Honda isn't worth—"

"Good-bye! There's another dealer down the street I want to talk to."

"Wait! Thousand, you said?"

After a half hour of paperwork, I enjoyed Harry's dexterous third count of the hundred dollar bills in his lap.

"Glad I had the title in glove compartment. Who'd ever thought . . ." His words trailed off.

The red light turned green and I stepped down on the Mustang's gas pedal, savoring the three seconds of squealing tires before we shot forward. Slowing as we caught up with heavier traffic, I glanced over at Harry's puzzled expression.

"What? Isn't it all there? I saw you counting—"

"An old junker," he interrupted. "How did you get him to pay this much for a junker and in cash?"

"Just a little dickering with a dickhead. Now, are you going to look for an apartment for me?"

"How can I do that without a car? You made me sell mine." He chuckled then laughed outright.

I slammed my hand on the stirring wheel. "I guess you'll have to take this one. I thought this was a stick, but it's an automatic. I hate automatics. I want something I can really shift and move with."

Harry grunted. "I know you ain't drunk anymore, so you gotta be nuts, Bob. I can't pay you back. How the hell would I even license this thing? And insurance. They demand insurance. Do you have any idea what the insurance would be? At least two months of my salary." He threw himself back in the seat and glared at me. "And, where I live, the goddamn car would be ripped off in twenty-four hours . . . tops."

"Make you a deal. As soon as we . . . find me . . . a place with a bed, I'll help locate a garage for the car, something with a strong lock. So, where do we start looking?"

Harry chewed his lower lips a minute. "You're serious. You are goddamn serious." He blew out a breath and straightened up. "But I don't play games. You're going in the wrong direction. You need to turn west."

My fingers opened and closed on the steering wheel. "Okay, Harry, no games. Let me be honest with you. I want an apartment in the middle of the lowest scum in town."

"Thanks." I didn't miss his sarcasm.

"After all this time, you know better, Harry. I've got to live in the area where . . ." My knuckles turned white on the wheel. ". . . where I can start looking for the son-of-a-bitch who killed Eileen." I heard him suck in breath. "I want to begin now, today."

When I looked at him this time, Harry wore a solemn, hard expression. In my gut, I knew he was seeing me as one determined bastard and that felt good. I relaxed my grip on the wheel.

"You ain't gonna like living where I do, but there's a place a couple blocks away. Heard the rent is about three fifty a month and it's a whole lot cleaner. No rats. Might have a roach or two, though, since they go with the area." He twitched a smile. "But, they got security locks on the front door and a garage below ground. First, though, since we're downtown, let's stop at Jake's Diner. They serve the kinda soup I said you need."

"So, you're not going to try to talk me out of stalking this guy?"

"Why? You want me to?"

"Whoever else I've talked to about it has tried."

"I learned a long time ago, never step in front of a man willing to give up everything to get someplace. In Vietnam that woulda gotten me killed. Young as I was, I learned to recognize the look."

"This isn't Vietnam."

"But things don't change much when it gets down to survival. This is just a different time, different place. Charley is still out there."

"You, ah, aren't going to have those . . . flash-backs, are you, Harry?"

"Naw. Not as long as I take my pills and keep away from booze." I gulped and flicked a glance at him. He wasn't smiling. He had stated fact. "Pull into that lot. We're at Jake's."

The shiny new car looked conspicuous in the vacant lot next to the weathered brick building. According to the faded and peeling words painted high on the wall, the structure had once been a business selling supplies to travelers in covered wagons. The "Dodge Street Outfitters" had long ago deteriorated to a dive serving food to customers with very little money and less dignity. Harry glanced back at the Mustang before stepping over the filthy drunk lying motionless on the diner's stoop.

We took seats at a battered, antique oak table near the entrance where we could still see the car through the streaked dirt of the bay window. I picked up the plastic-covered menu.

"What do you suggest?"

"You still feel like upchucking?"

"I'll be fine as long as I don't smell grease or cigar smoke. Never had a tolerance for either."

"Then order the chicken noodle soup."

"What are you having?"

"Chili."

"That sounds good."

"Not for you. The chili here would eat right through your gut and you'd be shitting blood for a week. Like the jogging, you gotta build up to it. So, you haven't answered me."

We stared at one another for a long moment. "About what?"

"How do you want me to pay you back . . . for the Mustang."

"So you are taking it."

He ignored my comment. "With overtime I only make seven hundred bucks a month. My ex-wife gets most of it."

"I didn't know you were married."

"Friends don't have to know everything, do they? She dumped me several years ago. Said she got tired of hearing me scream in the night. I have ten years to go on child support for my last kid. So . . . how do you want me to pay you back? You see, I'm no dummy. Nothing is a free ride. Not family, not friendship . . . and not that Mustang."

For the first time since looking at him over Eileen's body, I studied Harry's face. The shrapnel had left deep valleys and craters. Age lines flowed around the marks as if looking for room to wrinkle his appearance. The man behind that face would make an interesting portrait. I coughed to clear the fullness that rose in my throat. "Okay. Nothing is free, but . . . don't worry about it just now. Let me think it over."

Rushing past the line waiting to be seated, I checked my watch again. Damn it! Maggie probably thought I would not show and went home. The lobby inside Merrill's had filled to capacity.

"Excuse me," I muttered to a man who needed to skip a meal or two. Instead of shifting to allow me room, he turned, blocking my path. Our collision did not phase him. I, however, bounced back to where I had a head-to-toe view of him. His voice spoke a foot over my 5-10 frame as if he were addressing a child, "Now, you ain't cutting in front of me, sonny. I've been waiting an hour for a table."

I slowly tilted my head back, squared my shoulders, and glared into his piggish eyes. "I have reservations . . . and I'm late. You . . . will . . . excuse me."

"Don't think so. That lady up front ain't called no one in fifteen minutes, so you just go back outside and wait your turn."

I hadn't spent twenty-plus years with wealthy relatives for nothing. My finger beckoned him to bend closer. I lowered my voice. "Sir, I don't want anyone to hear, but I'm the reason no one has been seated for the past fifteen minutes."

"What?" He demanded in a disbelieving whisper.

"I'm the owner's son. I'm supposed to be up front seating guests, one special guest in particular." Finger beckoned. He leaned closer. "If I don't get up there, it will be another goddamn hour before you get to feed your fat face!"

With an indignant gasp, he jerked away, just enough for me to squeeze between him and a pretty blonde. He yelled "I don't like your attitude, mister, so you better find me a good table and fast!"

"So sue me!" I called back as I edged toward the "Wait to be Seated" sign.

With an armful of menus, a woman in a tasteful evening dress stood behind the barricade. She flashed a breathy smile, the reservation podium's light catching on her too-white teeth. Before she could speak, I asked "Table for Maggie Holmes?"

She blinked at her duties being anticipated, but quickly scanned the list of names. "Yes, Mrs. Holmes has been seated."

My gaze swept the large dining area crammed with tables, customers, and serving people. At the far wall sat the short, slender, middle-aged woman I recognized. Her eyes caught mine and she waved me forward. Something about her looked different. I remembered she always looked perfectly groomed, stylishly dressed, suiting her corporate role as a power secretary. Hair style. That's it. Her dark hair curled tightly about her head as if recently permed and too hurriedly styled.

I slid into the seat across from her, noting the cocktail and table setting obviously waiting for me. "I'm really sorry I'm late. I found an apartment this afternoon and the paperwork was slow."

"Quite all right, Mr. Norris. Seems everything's slow, including service here. I didn't get seated until twenty minutes ago. I went ahead and ordered, including your drink. Scotch and water. Correct?"

Air bubbled in my recovering stomach. "Good memory. Yes, thank you."

"Our meals should be here shortly. So, you've decided to move into an apartment so soon?" Her brown eyes looked too big over her glass of wine. She set down the glass, her fingers nervously tracing its shape.

"The house is too big, too full of memories . . . just plain too much for me now. I wanted a place where I could sleep, but not necessarily live in, if you know what I mean."

"Live in. Yes. I understand that. I live in a beautiful place, an apartment by Crazy Horse Lake. I've been there ten years. Ah, where did you decide to rent?"

"Towards the downtown area."

"Lots of renovation being done . . . in that area." The waitress arrived with the salads, which neither of us touched.

Sipping the Scotch, I couldn't help but notice how secluded our table seemed, backed into its own little corner, and wondered if it was Maggie's deliberate choice.

"Well, Mr. Norris," she lowered her voice a fraction and I naturally leaned forward. "Let's get down to business. Eileen gave me a copy of a file a few days before she died." Her eyes glistened with rising tears. She took a sip of wine and continued, "On-On the day she was murdered, she phoned me and-and wanted this file put in a safe place. Her instructions were 'Do not show it to anyone.' I locked the folder in the trunk of my car. I didn't even think of it again, let alone read it, until after her-her funeral . . . Mr. Norris, I don't know what to do with it now. If Bison Insurance learns of my part in hiding it, I could lose my job, and, if I go to the police, I know I would be fired for-for breaking a confidence or possibly something worse."

"Mrs. Holmes-Maggie, calm down. What is in the file?"

She wet her lips. "A Mr. Frank Harper is one of our Vice Presidents. He was Eileen's direct superior, and now mine, I guess. His wife passed away a few weeks ago. She had a five hundred thousand dollar life insurance policy. In the file . . ." her words came out in a rush, "Eileen investigated her own boss for insurance fraud, Mr. Norris!"

I leaned back as the waitress placed a plate with a medium rare rib-eye steak in front of me. I frowned at it. Apparently the ever-efficient Maggie knew even my steak preference and probably had a file of my likes and dislikes. As the small bowl of spinach was placed beside my plate I thought Aha! She screwed up! Then I heard "Miss, the spinach is mine. The corn goes to Mr. Norris." I tried to concentrate, but as I shifted in my chair I glimpsed the shapely legs of the waitress hesitating at another table.

Maggie pointedly cleared her throat bringing my attention back to her expectant stare. Yeah, she had notes on me all right! The Scotch disappeared in one swallow. "Quit with the Mr. Norris. You sound like one of my students. Call me Bob."

"Certainly. If you wish, since this should be less formal . . . I guess."

"Right. So, why can't you turn the file over to someone in the company?"

"I don't know who. I can't take it to lower management. Above me is the whole group of vice presidents, with Mr. Harper in the midst and directly in my path in the chain of command. Bison is known for the sincere loyalty of its management. In fact, the president and Mr. Harper are close friends. I would not be allowed access to the Board of Directors without going through Mr. Harper. And if my complicity leaked out . . . Any way you look at it, I would not be able to get another executive secretary job in this city."

"Is the file that incriminating?"

"Yes. It contains enough evidence to indict Mr. Harper." She fidgeted with her napkin then whispered. "In fact, it contains evidence he manipulated his wife into using an undetectable chemical that resulted in her death . . . so he could collect her insurance."

"Murder? You are describing murder and fraud. Why for God's sake did you call me?"

"I know how close you were with . . . your wife. I thought she may have told you some of this. I thought she may have mentioned what she was going to do with the file."

"You may know a lot about me, Maggie, and-and about my marriage, but one thing Eileen did not do at home was talk about her work. Nothing. Not one word about anything like this . . ." My thoughts raced. "Well . . . she did mention investigating an employee . . . and she was nervous and short-tempered that day . . . No, that's reaching. No, this is all news to me. Wow. So, this file would be damned important if there's no other record . . . Wait. I got the impression Eileen did most of her work by computer. Would there be a computer file, too?"

"I thought of that, too and it worries me. But no one knows her access number, not even me. It's five digits of two letters and three numbers. Have-Have you seen it written down someplace?"

"No! Why the hell would she write it down?"

"It does change every two weeks. I thought maybe somewhere in her purse. Oh, the men who . . . the men at the store, they didn't get her purse did they?" She clutched my hand. "If someone got their hands on that code and knew what it was . . . they could find the file and erase it. Mr. Harper could get that money. He'd go free. Bob, I have to find that code to change it and protect the file . . . until I can get to the Board."

"Why don't you give me the file with the paperwork on everything. I'll look through Eileen's things for the code. Give me your phone number so I can let you know if I find it." She fumbled in her small clutch for a notepad and pencil stub.

I stared at my now-cold steak. "What is preventing Harper from getting his money right now?"

"There is a flag put on files under investigation. If Eileen was the one to flag it, only her code will release the file to payment."

"Can't a VP do pretty much anything he wants in the company?"

"Perhaps after a few weeks of file inactivity. Or someone could be appointed to replace Eileen and take over her workload. They could remove the flag. That will take at least another two weeks because the Board has to approve upper management appointments."

"Wouldn't the replacement find what Eileen found?"

"Maybe, but Vicky Templeton is the most likely candidate. She's, ah, rumored to be friendly . . . almost intimate with Mr. Harper, even before his wife's death."

Chapter Four

At the crest of the short incline, the house stood dark. The full moon broke through the scattered clouds, but soon disappeared behind a large, thick one. The street lights barely filtered through the trees and shrubbery on the front lawn.

I pushed the button on my watch. A green light filled the face. I had twenty minutes before I had to pick up Harry at his new Stop-and-Go. His shift ended at 11:30. We were moving his things to my apartment.

I parked the Mustang behind the Ferarri. Judge Williams had left a message on my answering machine I accessed by my cell phone. Urgent business had come up, so he hadn't been able to move the Ferrari into my garage. I stared at its rear window, wondering if I really wanted to move it myself. The thought of Eileen's perfume inside the car unnerved me. Would her accusing image appear in the car when I climbed behind its wheel? Bad enough in my dreams, but if I were trapped in such a small space . . . .

Fear struck me in such a way I had to force myself to leave the Mustang and walk toward the house, another place I didn't want to enter, but I had nothing at the new apartment. I needed clothes and toiletry items. My hand inserted the key. It grated in the lock. I slid my hand around the door frame and turned on the lights. Surely, ghost don't appear in well-lit rooms. Still, I ran from place to place grabbing and stuffing things in garbage sacks. They held more than luggage, anyway.

As I threw three bulging garbage bags into the Mustang's back seat, I remembered my paints and canvases. The door had slammed with the locking behind me. Tomorrow in the day light would be soon enough. Nothing was that important, except . . . .

I had told Maggie I would look through Eileen's things for that damn code. My eyes focused on the Ferrari. Maggie had mentioned Eileen's purse. I remembered Eileen stuffing it under her seat.

Almost in slow motion, I unlocked the passenger door and opened it. The dome light came on. Nothing else appeared.

Holding my breath in anticipation of her perfume, I pulled the purse out and dumped it in the seat. My goose bumps lessened as I grew more intent on searching through the last things she had touched. The small sticky pad at the top of the pile had lines of printing indenting its top note. Eileen had fiddled with the notepad then the visor mirror before we went . . . I pulled down the visor and there it was stuck to the mirror, the note with a five digit code written in Eileen's handwriting. "France's Amour" floated to me. I merely sighed, suddenly relieved rather than afraid.

The front door lock clicked and I rushed inside to use that phone. I didn't want to risk a cell phone interception on this call. After several rings, I heard Maggie's tired voice. "What is it?"

"Maggie? This is Bob."

"Bob?"

"Bob Norris."

"Oh! I'm sorry, Bob. I must have dozed off."

"You woke me. My turn to get you up. I found the access code."

"What? Wonderful! Do you want to bring it here or have me meet you—"

"Just get a pencil and paper. An executive secretary does have those, doesn't she?"

"Ah, you're teasing . . . Okay, I'm ready."

"B-N-6-1-5."

"Wonderful. Oh, I said that. Anyway, first thing tomorrow I'll get to the file, encrypt it somewhere else, and start searching for access to someone on the Board. Where can I reach you?"

"I know you've got my cell phone number in your little file, but don't use it. Too easy for someone else to overhear. And don't leave a message on the answering machine here at the house. Someone might break in again and listen to that. As soon as I get a phone at the apartment, I'll call you at your home number."

"Fine. Well, goodbye and thanks for sharing this burden."

"No, I'm the one who's grateful. Now I know where I'm headed and that Eileen wants me going there."

"What?"

"Never mind. Talk to you soon."

The match's flame caught the corner of the note. I dropped it into the kitchen sink then turned on the faucet. The ashes mixed with the running water and swirled down the drain. I calmly walked out the front door and smiled as the lock sounded behind me.

Since I was late, I expected to find Harry waiting. Instead he stood behind the counter of his new Stop-and-Go, stocking cigarettes in the overhead rack.

"Sorry, Bob. Overnight man called in. I gotta work another shift."

"Let the manager come in."

"I'm elected since I'm the new man and I need the money. Remember?"

"What time are you getting off?"

"Six, if my day relief comes in on time."

"I'll be in bed. Here's your key. You get the bedroom next to the bathroom. Don't wake me. Got a feeling I'm going to sleep well tonight, for the first time in many nights."

"Hey, I'll stay another day in my old place. I told you I don't really need to move, anyway."

"Harry! Harry!" I moaned. "We've been over this time and again. You can't afford that dump. I have the space. That one bedroom is bigger than your whole goddamn apartment. Get off work in the morning, come on over, get some sleep . . . then we'll move your stuff. It's decided. I will see your sweet face when I wake up, right?"

"Yeah, I'll be there."

I opened the door.

"Wait!" I looked back. "Be careful with my car."

Three blocks later I arrived at my new place of residence. The furnished apartment occupied a quarter of the second floor in a spacious two-story brick building. I had three bedrooms, bathroom, kitchen, separate dining room, and airy living room. Plus I had negotiated for two parking spaces in the secured underground garage. Harry's Mustang would be safe.

With a garbage bag slung over each shoulder, I trudged up the stairs. On the second flight was much easier, mainly because I had a pair of well-shaped feminine legs climbing the stairs in front of me. Her thighs rubbed together and, with each sway of upward motion, her fanny peeked from under a wonderfully short skirt. When we reached the hallway, my attention stayed on the hip-movement. I stopped at my door and could only blink in surprise when she turned.

"You following me, mister?"

The bags slid to the floor, as I took in her brown calf-eyes, then the leather halter top's exposure of abundant flesh. Her hand brushed long blonde hair over a slender shoulder. Huffing a short breath of impatience, she cocked her head. The pouting lips gave her a little-girl appearance, but the total picture put my guess that she was around twenty.

"I . . . Ah, I'm going to my place. Here . . . right here." Without looking away, I shoved one hand into my pocket for the keys.

"Oh?" She leaned forward a fraction and lowered her voice. "You just moving in?"

"Yeah . . . Yes. Here. Right here."

A smile parted those glossed lips. "Then I guess we're neighbors. This is my door . . . across from yours."

I managed to swallow. "Really. I'm Bob Norris. Do you live with your parents?"

Her bubbly laugh echoed in the hall. "You're giving me a line, right?"

"A line? No. You're young, so I thought your family . . . What's your name, anyway?"

"Call me Lori, just Lori. And, no, I don't live with anyone, except sometimes my man comes over. Don't even know where my parents are. Wait. I take that back. My old man's serving time. Been there fifteen years."

"Oh. Oh, I'm sorry to hear that." I glanced down at the keys I nervously jingled. "Well, Lori . . . nice to have met you. Please excuse me. I've got a lot of stuff to put away and it's late."

She looked at the two lumpy black bags.

"Need help?"

"No, but thanks anyway. I can get it. I've still got another bag in the car. Lots of stuff to put away."

"Is your place furnished?"

"Yeah, but I'll replace it someday with better stuff."

"I rent mine furnished, too. Yours is probably just like mine. I could start unpacking those while you get the other bag. Save you some time . . . since it is late."

I stared at the key I had inserted in the door lock. Why the hell not, Norris? "Sure, if you have the time."

My fingers flicked on the yellow glow of light as the girl rushed past me. She looked things over, nodding.

"Everything's just the same as my place. I could walk blindfolded and know where I'm at."

"That's good, I guess. I, ah, don't have any coffee to offer you. If you give me a few minutes, I could run down to that corner grocery and get a few things. It's open all night."

She giggled. "Yeah, I know. Don't do that. I just stopped by my place for a pack of cigarettes. I can take a few minutes, but I have to get back to work."

"You work this late? It's after twelve. What job keeps a young girl out this late?"

"You really are kidding me, right? You have no idea what I do?"

She held her arms out and slowly turned in place for me to better assess her appearance, I guess. Standing about five-eight, well-proportioned, barely clad, the girl certainly couldn't be a waitress at an area diner like Jake's. She was pretty enough to be an entertainer. I tried to remember if I had seen any bars or nightclubs nearby.

"I'm sorry, Lori. I'm not good at guessing games. Whatever you do, I bet you're good at it."

She frowned in disbelief, then a slow smile brought back her youthful appeal. "Yeah, that's what I've been told. Maybe sometime you'll see me at work. Well, time's a wastin' and we didn't get any unpacking done, but I gotta go. I'll be back in a couple of hours. See ya!"

An hour later, I had my clothes hung and stood staring at the bed mattress and its questionable stains. Flipping it over only revealed more stains. Finally, I tore the garbage bags and spread them over the bed as temporary sheets. Stretching out, I considered where I would buy a new bed in the morning. With each move, the crackling plastic irritated my nerves, but I drifted off to sleep hoping it prevented the little creatures in the mattress from crawling onto my body.

A woman's scream awakened me. That was something new to my dreams. The past few nights I had dreamt of Eileen in a rowboat. She hated boats and fishing. But in the dream, I sat opposite her holding a fishing rod. Each time I reacted to a tug on the line, she leaned over with a pair of scissors and cut it. She never said anything, let alone screamed.

The scream came again, only this time more of a screech. I sat up, fully awake now. Thumps came from the hallway outside my door. Pulling blue jeans over my underwear, I stepped bare-footed into the shadowed strangeness of my new apartment. Torn blinds hung at an angle across the wide double windows of the living room. The street's dim light slanted through the blinds, barely marking the dark and ragged furniture. Another screech kick-started my attention back to the hall. A woman's voice shouted a long list of creative profanity. Sounds like Lori. She knows more cuss words than even Harry. I pulled the door open, but knew better than to step into that hall.

A broad-shouldered man stood with his back to me. He filled the open doorway across from mine. Easing my door partially closed, I watched through a less obvious few inches of space.

"You bitch!" The male voice boomed. "You give me two hundred dollars or you're dead meat! You understand?"

"Fuck you!" Lori shouted back. "Get outta here 'cause I don't owe you shit!"

"Two hundred!" He planted beefy hands on the door frame as if he would force it wider and launch himself forward.

"For what?" she snidely demanded.

That girl's no coward! And, for some insane reason, I opened my door a little wider.

"I sent you six johns! My math says you owe me another two

hundred. Or can't you count, bitch?"

"Bullshit! You might have had six johns, but I only did four tricks. They ain't gonna to pay, if they don't do nothing!"

Lori's a prostitute? She's too young and pretty for whoring! Damn! What's going on here?

One of the man's big hands whipped to his back pocket. He yanked upwards and the hall light reflected off metal.

Chrome! A weapon! No, goddamn it! I won't let you kill her!

Turning, my hand hit the back of a wooden chair. I grabbed it by the legs and rushed into the hall. Using my body's momentum, I swung the chair up and slammed it down over the man's head and shoulders. Wood splintered in all directions. He dropped where he stood, a muffled gun blast sounding under him as he hit the floor. I stared at the heels of his shiney, black Busters. Where would he get those? Probably a discount store.

"Hey! Bob!"

I looked up at Lori. She smiled and lit a cigarette with steady hands.

"Lori. Are you, ah, all right?"

"I'm fine," she said, shifting from side to side to assess the man on the floor. She blew smoke from her nose. "But Alabama there is either hurting real bad or dead."

"Alabama?"

"Yeah. On the floor in front of you? My man. Or, as you would call him, my pimp. Well, He-man, let's get him all the way in here before one of the other neighbors come looking."

Totally numb, I stepped across the unmoving form and into her living room. Grasping handfuls of his suitcoat, I leaned back and pulled. Since he was heavier than anticipated, I only moved him a few inches. With a disgusted sigh, Lori unceremoniously rolled him over, bent one of his knees then the other, then slammed her door shut. His legs flopped like a frog's, but I barely noticed. I morbidly watched the red stain spreading across his shirt front. My gaze flew to the fingers still wrapped around the handle of the gun.

"Tape. Lori, do you have any tape?"

"Tape? Well, somewhere, I guess. What the hell for?"

"To hold his wrists together . . . like tying him before he wakes up."

She took a long drag of her cigarette. "Had me worried. I thought you wanted to tape up that bullet hole. Bob! He's dead. Looks like he shot himself as he fell."

Cold sweat instantly beaded on my forehead. My stomach rolled. "Dead? I didn't kill him. I just hit him with a chair. He was trying to kill you."

"Take a good look, fella. His eyes are open and he ain't moving. What does he look like to you?"

The image of me standing behind bars flashed across my mind. The sick feeling in my stomach migrated up to the back of my throat. My mouth moved, but no words formed. I stepped close enough to the wall to lean my back against it.

"Police," I finally mumbled. "We have to call the police. Where's your phone?"

Lori stubbed out her cigarette. "You ain't calling shit! Just rest there and let me think." She left me alone with him for a few moments then reappeared with a wadded towel and a heavy skillet. She set the towel on the blood stain, then pressed the skillet on top of it. "I'm not having him bleed all over the place." I nodded. She lit another cigarette. "We got to get this goddamn body out of my apartment."

"But he's dead and I . . . Well, I have to talk to the police. See, I never killed anyone before. Doesn't that upset you? You act like you see this shit every day."

"No, not every day. This is the second pimp I've had in less than two years. Alabama shot and killed my other man. Tonight was his turn to go. And I want the dead son-of-a-bitch out of here!"

"Why can't the police handle it?" It was uncharacteristic for me to whine, yet I wasn't exactly feeling myself, either.

"Because, He-man, I would go to jail. If I go to jail, you can be sure I'll take you with me."

"But, I was protecting you! I didn't mean to kill him."

"Think the cops would believe that story? You really are a hayseed, ain't you? Listen to me real careful like. You call the police.

They come here. They'll see a dead pimp on the floor and a whore with her john. The whore, me, and the john, you, get arrested. Since we ain't got money to defend ourselves, it would be a kangaroo court. And—" She snapped her fingers. I flinched. "—twenty years in the big house!"

"I-I have money. I can get the best lawyer in the city."

"Yeah, sure. If you're so rich, why is it you're moving into this dump?"

My reasons were sound. Lori's train of thought registered as melodramatic nonsense. I shook my head and pinched my eyes shut, working to see her perception of reality. Once I got beyond my own horror of the accident, I realized she was right. In this sordid world I had deliberately stepped into, she was absolutely right. My only choice was to play along with the role I had chosen.

I looked hard at the body on the floor. The man was a murderer, scum. What difference will it make if I tell the police about this incident? Who would be better off and who would be worse off? Stepping away from the wall, I assessed his body mass.

"He must weigh over two hundred. I'll need some help."

"Oh, sure. I'll just call a few neighbors over. I'm surprised someone hasn't offered already. Should I go knock on the doors of the other two apartments up here?"

Our eyes clashed over the body. "Well, Miss Smarty, I guess you don't know everything. The landlord told me one guy's off visiting someplace and the other renter moved out. Work's being done on the four apartments on the first floor, so they are empty. You're real observant, aren't you?"

She shrugged and looked bored. "Across the alley, across the street. Neighbors is neighbors."

"What time is it?" I demanded.

"A little after six. Why?"

"Harry will be home soon. He'll know what to do."

"Who the hell is Harry?"

"He's sharing my apartment."

"Your lover?"

"God, no! He's a friend who needs a place to stay."

44

Her pretty little shoulders shrugged again. "You want a cup of coffee while me wait?"

Coffee? I just killed somebody and had to think up how to hide the body. Yet, I'm suppose to drink coffee in the same room with the corpse?

"I don't think so."

"Well, I'm getting a cup. You're so damn polite I thought I'd offer." She paused. "Hey, someone's coming up the stairs."

I listened. "I don't hear anyone. Wait. What if it's one of those other men he was sending to you? You stay back. I'll check."

"Goddamn it! Just open the door and see if you recognize the bastard." She disappeared into the kitchen.

I stepped high over the unmoving fifty dollar suit, but my trailing foot caught on the angled arm. Noisily stumbling against the closed door, I cursed my clumsiness. The latch rasped as I turned the knob. Harry stood at our door trying to fit the unfamiliar key into the lock.

"Psst, Harry! Over here!"

He turned, looked back then frowned at me. "Didn't we rent this pad?"

"Yeah, but I want to see you first."

When he was close to the doorway, I opened it wider, grabbed his empty, pinned-up sleeve and pulled hard. As he staggered pass me, I checked the hallway. It was as empty as Harry's sleeve. Quickly shutting the door, I turned to face Harry's stunned expression.

"Sh-h-h! Keep your voice down, Harry. The guy's dead."

He wrinkled his nose, eyeing the skillet and towel on Alabama's chest. "What makes you think so, Bob?"

"He hasn't moved since I hit him."

Lori stuck her head out of the kitchen doorway. "You want a cup of coffee, Harry?"

His mouth dropped open. "Ah, hello, Lori. Long time no see."

"Hello, yourself. I, ah, remembered your voice and then the face. You were a john Alabama sent me, oh, three-four weeks ago, over on 10th. Right?"

"Wait, wait, wait!" I called out. "I don't want to hear the details. Harry, you spent money you couldn't afford on a woman?"

"Mind your own business!" Lori interrupted. "Harry and I didn't do it!"

His scarred expression quickly changed from indignant to humorous disbelief. "Oh, yeah! Look at you, Mister Clean! All you got on is a pair of pants in the middle of a girl's apartment with a stiff on the floor. You want me . . . to explain—"

I stopped him. "Lori's right. It's none of my business."

I closed my eyes, rolled my shoulders, and tried to rub some coherent thoughts through my scalp and into my frazzled brain. "None of . . . this . . . was my business. I should have stayed in that apartment across the hall and let him shoot her." My finger pointed at the girl now leaning against the kitchen doorframe. "I could have simply heard the shot and saw nothing. But, no, I opened my door. Now, Harry," I laid my hand on his shoulder. "we've got a problem. I hit that man who now lies dead on the floor of an accidental, but self-inflicted gunshot wound. I want to call the police. Lori wants to hide the body. You can be more objective. What should we do?"

Harry knelt at Alabama's shoulder. He pressed his fingertips into the side of the thick neck, then bent closer to the marbled eyes. "Yup, he's dead. When the cops hear this one is gone, they will surely party. You might even get a medal, Bob."

"Quit clowning. This is serious. What should we do?"

"Okay. You didn't kill him. He fell on his own gun. From all the splinters in the hall, I'd say you demolished whatever you hit him with." I nodded. "Had to hit him pretty hard to do that."

"He was going to shoot Lori!"

"Well, then you, Bob, ain't going to jail."

"What?" Lori's expression turned nasty. "You know those damn cops! They just come here, they'll bust me. I don't want to do time. And, you know, the judge would put me away, 'cause it was promised."

Harry studied her a moment, his face softening. "You on parole?"

"Yeah, you a cop?"

"No, or I would have taken you in last time we met. Right? But I do know a little about the law. What are you up for?"

"When Alabama shot my first man, I took the rap. Only got a year 'cause I had a clean record. Alabama got me a good lawyer who persuaded the jury I was protecting myself."

"That pretty much settles it." Harry stood and turned to me. "What were you thinking of doing?"

"Wait a minute. You're saying she would go to jail, for sure?"

"Yeah."

"Then let's get the body out of here."

Harry considered Alabama a long moment then walked to the window and palmed it open. He leaned out, looked all around, then turned to us, mumbling "It might just work."

"What will work?"

He looked at Lori. "Do you have something we can wrap him in. Make him look like a piece of furniture?"

"Make that look like furniture?" When he didn't laugh, she glanced around then shrugged. "He pays for this place. I'm only in and out. I haven't bought anything to make it . . . lived in. What do you have in mind?"

"I think we can get him out this morning."

"Harry!" I threw up my hands in frustration. "It's daytime out there. Someone will see us! Those neighbors she talked about, for example?"

"Not if we put the body in something, something that would contain furniture." He jerked back toward the window. "Wait! I thought I saw a crate next to the dumpster down the alley." He leaned out. "Yeah, it's there alright! A big one! Look at it."

I replaced him at the window. There stood the pale, wood-braced cardboard container beside the dirty blue of the trash bin. "How in the hell are we going to get something that size up here?"

"Look up! See the post sticking out from the roof with the pulleys? That's to haul big furniture up 'cause the old-fashioned stairs are too narrow. Lots of old buildings are rigged with 'em. We get a rope and rent a pickup. The crate should just fit through this wide window. Body in the crate, crate in the truck, dump the crate somewhere. Simple."

The excitement began to build inside me. This could work. "Where will we dump it?"

"Can you wait until we get to that point?"

Chapter Five

Lori and Harry stood beside me in front of Jake's. After a lunch of fat-soaked cheeseburgers, we took turns belching. Of course, Lori wasn't quite as obvious as Harry and me. We discussed the weather and the city's attempts to renovate downtown as Lori puffed a cigarette. Finally, she dropped the butt and we headed toward the Mustang. The crated Alabama waited at the apartment for his final trip.

As my two new cohorts headed into the apartment building, I walked off to look for a pickup truck to rent. Three blocks later I found Honest Jasper's. The rental business had obviously occupied the building at 20th and Howard for a very long time. Standing in the doorway viewing the junk-filled shelves and counters, I believed the sign out front that read "Jasper will rent you everything!" The rotund, jovial Jasper told me he could provide me with anything from a flea farm to a diesel train engine. I gave him a hundred dollar deposit on the ten year old beat-up Dodge pickup parked in his storage lot, alongside that damn train engine.

I backed the rust-tinged gray truck into the alley behind our building. Lori sat in her window. She waved and I waved back. Just above her, a skinny hemp rope dangled from the roof's pulley, it's end curving up like Lori's faint smile.

I just reached the spot directly below the window when a single loud pop bounced off the alley walls. Gunshot! I jammed my foot on the brake and threw myself across the seat. Over my thundering heartbeat, I heard Lori's laughter filtering in the truck window. The vehicle continued to roll. I cautiously sat up and pulled the emergency brake. Peering up at Lori, I couldn't believe she was laughing so hard she had to wipe tears from her eyes. Damn, she's got a weird sense of humor!

"Did you do that?" I yelled.

"You just rolled over a plastic bottle! No one's shooting at you! Hey, Harry, Bob thinks a bottle just shot him!"

Climbing from the truck, I kept my face down so she wouldn't see how red it was. A coiled end of the rope hit me on the head. That's what I got for not paying attention. Harry had replaced Lori in the window.

"Pick that up. I'll tell you when to pull," he called down then grabbed the other, dangling end above him and took it with him as he ducked back. I put on the leather gloves I had bought, not rented, from Jasper.

"Pull slow!" Harry's voice ordered from deep inside Lori's apartment.

As soon as the slack had been taken up, I had to really grip and strain to move hand-over-hand. This feels like more than two hundred pounds. The crate! Okay, I'm hauling three hundred. High overhead, squeaks sounded as the strained hemp moved through the wooden block and tackle. Sweat trickled but I didn't let go as several feet of rope piled at my feet. When I heard a loud groaning scrape, I looked up to see the crate edging out the window. It teetered on the ledge with Lori's hands on the near side and Harry's strained face looking over the top as he pushed and guided, too.

Alabama's container slid from the windowsill and swung into the air, directly over the truck bed. Slowly, I let the rope slip across my leather gloves, clamping my hold to control the crate's decent. The good intentions didn't work. The box began to fall faster. I leaned back, the thin rope almost cutting through my gloves. Suddenly, the strain was gone, dropping me on my ass.

"Pulley broke! Damn!" Harry shouted down, as I stared up at the fast-approaching crate. It hit the truck bed with a crash and splintering echoes. The Dodge rocked on its suspension. I jumped to my feet to peer over its side.

The crate had broken open around Alabama. He lay sprawled, not really looking any worse than he had before.

When Harry and Lori rushed to my side, I was still staring at the catastrophe.

Lori stretched on tip-toe. "Hell, the fall didn't hurt him none!"

"My thoughts exactly," I quipped. "Harry, I think I'd better run to a hardware store and buy a tarp to cover all this."

"There's plastic hanging out of the dumpster. We'll use that!"

"No, no, no! We need something heavier, darker. If we get stopped, the cops can see through that stuff!"

Lori wandered around to the back of the bin, eyeing a couch bound for the dump. She tugged on it, her butt rounding tightly against the thin denim of her jeans. "Let's throw . . . this on top of him."

Twenty minutes later, the three of us stared through the windshield as I drove east on Farnum Street in the general direction of the Missouri River. "Now, that we're on our way, Harry, where are we going?"

"I'm still thinking."

"What the hell—"

"I got an idea!" Lori interrupted. "Harry, do you know Fox?"

"I know Fox," he ground out.

"Alabama and Fox have been fighting over turf for the past couple years. Let's dump him in Fox's lap."

At the red light, I turned to her. She actually looked almost normal in the jeans and over-sized T-shirt. Except for the marijuana plant painted on the shirt. And her hair looked different. Now, dark shiny brown, shoulder length, parted in the middle and hanging straight around her clean face. What happened to the long, blonde, curly hair?

Harry interrupted my assessment. "Didn't know the two of them was fighting. Not a bad idea there, Lori. Give Bob the directions he's so worried about!"

I was soon backing into another cluttered alley. The vacant warehouses on each side towered six stories above us. Pigeons flew in and out of broken windows. "Shouldn't we wait until dark for this?" I spoke as I strained to look over one shoulder and watch where I was backing. "Someone might see us dumping him."

"These buildings been empty for ten years. The only people around here are winos and they ain't gonna admit to seeing this. No one sees them, they don't see no one."

"Still makes me nervous." I pulled to a stop. "Lori, why don't you keep an eye out while Harry and I get this done?"

"The he-man has turned back into a scaredy cat . . . again." More than her words, the echo of her loud laugh made me cringe.

I lowered the tailgate as Harry untied the pulley rope we had used to lash down the plastic covering the sofa and the dead pimp under it. Hoping I didn't step on Alabama again, I edged around the over-turned sofa and hefted the far end. Harry gripped the other armrest through the ripped fabric, his hand disappearing in the cotton stuffing. I pushed while he pulled. This is working!

Then Harry lost his grip. The sofa hit the ground so hard, its wooden frame broke, tearing Harry's armrest away from the sofa back. It took the both of us to wiggle the damn thing off the tailgate. Finally, it slammed onto the ground, broken and even more pathetic than when we found it. In the middle of the alley like that, it looked appropriately abandoned.

Now it was Alabama's turn. Standing on each side of couch, Harry grabbed one foot and I grabbed the other. Much easier than the sofa, the corpse slid out and dropped in place, nicely sprawled on the piece of broken furniture.

Lori came back from her corner lookout post. She shook her head. "Naw. He looks too relaxed. Sit him up." With a bit of huffing and puffing, we accomplished that. "Cross that leg over this one." Then her hands deftly searched his coat pockets. She held up his wallet and a fat cigar. After sticking the cigar into his mouth, wedging it between his back teeth to hold it in place, she pointed at the gun lying in the truck bed's debris. Harry retrieved that, wiped off his prints with the end of Alabama's coat and settled the weapon on the corpse's lap. One more pass of Lori's hands over the suitcoat and she came up with a thick money roll. First, she counted out three thousand dollars, then she tossed the remaining substantial roll to Harry. His one-handed catch was admirable. "Keep it," Lori told him. "Alabama ain't gonna need it!"

Harry looked like she had clubbed him right between the eyes. "Why don't you take all of it?"

"This is what he stole from me. What's in your hand, ain't mine."

Harry stuffed the wad back in Alabama's pocket. "I've never robbed the dead, not in Nam, not anywhere. I ain't startin' now."

Relieved to be back in heavy traffic and with an empty truck bed, I glanced at Lori. "Where to?"

"Back to my place. I'll have to pack and move."

"What are you talking about?"

"My apartment belonged to Alabama. I ain't got a job no more. No pimp, no work. I can't walk the streets by myself."

"Why can't you find a job as a waitress or hotel clerk or some-thing?

"Bob, you're sounding like a hayseed again. I've worked the streets since I was fourteen. Ten years. Ten years of working for pimps. Everyone knows me. Once Fox spreads the word that Alabama's dead, some other man will find me."

"Are you using . . . like hooked?" Harry quickly asked.

"Not since my last dry out, a year ago when I served time. Alabama quit trying to force shit on me. Knew I was pissed at him. But, my next man will probably crank me up. So what? That's the least of my worries. Right now, I need a place to stay."

I tried to think through all she had said in so few words. Her per-spective was so different, so foreign to me, yet just what I needed right now. Entering an intersection on a red light, I barely missed a collision and prayed a cop hadn't seen that one. "Why don't you stay with me. There's a third bedroom. It would be a perfect place for you to hide out, rest up, whatever."

Her silence bothered me, but not as much as the narrow-eyed assessment I glimpsed from both people beside me.

"No, I can't."

"Why?"

"Are you going to pimp for me?"

"Of course not!" I floored it through a yellow light. "I'm going to make sure you stay off the streets . . . if that's what you want. You will never have to sell yourself again."

"I've heard this crap before! I know how it works. You keep me around for a few weeks and as soon as you get low on money . . . or your wife decides she wants you back, I'll find my ass on the streets again!"

"He ain't like that, Lori!" Harry put in. "First off, Bob's got more money than he knows what to do with. Second, his wife is dead."

"Dead? She shifted in the seat like it was uncomfortable. "So, you're living with him now. And the two of you want me to move in. I get it. You're some kind of perverts. Well, I'll charge a hundred extra for a three-some. I've seen it done, but I ain't never—"

"Why don't you just shut up!" I shouted. "I don't want to hear about . . . what you've seen or what you've done! All I want is to offer you a place to stay. No sexual favors or money exchange. If you . . . want that from me or Harry, then forget it! But . . ." I glared at the car in front of me like it was the enemy, my fingers white on the wheel. "Well, the extra bedroom is still yours, even if you can't change. You just keep your johns away from our apartment, away from me. Understand?"

My anger must have impressed my two passengers. When I glanced at them, both stared straight ahead, carefully ignoring everything but their thoughts. No one spoke, even when we left the truck parked beside the Mustang in our building's underground garage. Only the creaking and clicking of the old elevator broke the silence as we rode up. When the doors opened on the second floor, Harry and I hesitated long enough for Lori to exit first. She went directly to Alabama's apartment door, unlocked it, and slammed it behind her. Harry kept glancing at her door as he unlocked ours, but still didn't comment.

Trying to find a comfortable position on the lumpy couch seat, I listened to Harry getting a glass of water in the kitchen. Finally, he returned and straddled a wooden chair facing me.

He shook his head before sighing heavily. "So, when are you taking the truck back?"

"I thought I'd keep it for a few days. Need to haul some more stuff and we have your things to move."

"Like I said, I ain't got much. So, right now can I use the car? I need to pay my child support at the Court House."

"It's your car. What are you asking me for?"

"Yeah, you told me, but I don't even have a set of keys."

"Sorry." I dug in my pocket. "I got two sets. Here!" I tossed a key ring toward him and he grabbed it right out of the air with that one strong hand. "All yours! And, you know what? I'm not going to miss it a bit. I like driving that truck. I think I'll go shopping for one."

"Don't think I'm driving you to the car dealer. You'd probably sell the Mustang from under me!"

"Harry! That hurts!" I chided him. We grinned at one another. A knock interrupted our exchange.

"Who would come visiting? Nobody I know has my address. You expecting anybody?" I demanded.

"Hell, no!" Harry snapped. "People I know wouldn't knock polite-like."

"Could it be one of Alabama's friends?"

"How the hell would I know that? Think I'm Superman and can see through the door?"

"Of course not. But, you can go see who it is."

"Why me? 'Cause I'm the tough guy? You killed the pimp!"

"It was an accident!"

"That you made happen!"

Another knock.

"Oh, never mind. Come in!" Harry shouted.

"They can't. It's locked," I told him in a loud whisper.

"So, go unlock it! It's your place!"

He didn't bother to even stand as I went by. You're the combat veteran and I'm answering the door. He just shrugged at my disgusted expression.

The distorted view through the peep hole revealed no one waiting in the shadowed hallway. I clicked the lock and cautiously eased the door open.

"Hi!" Lori's greeting startled me. She leaned against the wall next to my door, a suitcase in one hand, a filled garbage bag at her feet. When I only stared, she stood up, her gaze studying the hall's thread-bare carpeting. "Well, ah, is the bedroom still available?"

I worked real hard not to smile. "Nobody's applied for it in the past ten minutes." When she looked up with hope in those big eyes, I let the smile show. "So, I guess, you want it?"

"I thought it over . . . all the way back. Standing there in Alabama's place, I realized you and Harry are probably all right. I mean, you handled Alabama okay and everything."

"Thanks."

Her neck arched with returning pride. "I can come and go as I want, but no johns, right?"

"Right."

"You give me any crap and I'm outta here, okay?"

"Okay. You won't get any from us . . . as long as you follow the rules."

"Rules? More rules than 'No johns'?"

"Not right now, but we'll have to see. Maybe we can all make them up as we go along. Is this all your stuff?" I started to reach for the garbage bag, but she hefted it.

"I'll get this. You can carry my TV over. Door's open."

As protective as she was of that bag, I sure hoped it didn't contain anything dangerous or drugs. The bag bumped me as she awkwardly entered the apartment. I noticed she let Harry take the damn thing, then I turned to get her TV.

An hour later, Harry and I tried to concentrate on the image on Lori's TV, as our shower sounded in the background. We pretended an exaggerated interest in the fine art of adjusting the antenna. The blurred reception remained, no matter how it was positioned. The end table beneath the set wobbled every time one of us touched it. Just as I knelt to look under the table, we heard the bar of soap bouncing on the shower floor. My face reddened as I identified missing screws from the table leg, and thought of looking up bare feminine legs.

"Gotta replace this furniture," I mumbled.

"Why not? You can buy anything you damn please!" Harry aimed the remote control and thumbed the channel button.

"Wait! Turn it back. That channel had early news."

"So read the papers! There's got to be a good movie someplace."

The shower scene from *Psycho* appeared. Harry and I glanced at one another, then at the bathroom wall with our own shower just beyond. He punched the remote and found a game show, something I always hated. I picked up a worn paperback with no cover left by the last tenant and was soon lost in the first chapter. Involved in terrorists from the Middle East plotting to blow up an airplane on an international flight, I vaguely registered Lucy and Ricky fighting on one side of me and the shower shutting off on the other.

As I started the last page, I felt someone reading over my shoulder. My eyes met Lori's then moved down. She was wrapped in only a towel. Her slender hand shoved a glass of iced tea at me. I took a quick swallow to relieve my dry mouth. It didn't help. Between the dark, wet hair framing her face and the towel slipping down the curve of one plump breast, I was a mess. I shifted to conceal my instant arousal. Out of the corner of my eye, I saw Harry's mouth hanging open.

"Okay, time for a rule," I sputtered. "Listen up, Harry. Everyone will be properly dressed outside the bathroom and their own bedroom."

Lori frowned. She looked at Harry. "You agree with that one? I mean, like we're voting here."

Harry's mouth snapped shut. He hesitated, met my hard stare, then shrugged. "Yeah . . . I think so."

She pulled a straight-back chair from the dining room table and sat down, her knees modestly together and angled just enough to the side to allow the towel to part a little. "This is weird and I'm confused. I wasn't even going to charge you, one at a time that is. I guess, I was reading the wrong signals. If I'm not here for . . . that . . . for you, why am I here?"

I rubbed my hand over my face. Why can't anything I do be simple? This nobility crap isn't even close! "You were in trouble. I made it worse. Harry and I are just trying to do the neighborly thing, without any expectations. I don't know what signals we gave you. Now, get this clear. We are not interested in having sex with you. Right, Harry?"

Harry nodded his head then shook it. "That's right. I mean, no we ain't. I mean, what Bob says goes. You don't have to worry about us, Lori."

"Okay," she responded, but still didn't sound convinced. "What's going on here anyway? I'm no dummy. I been reading people mosta my life. When Harry said you got money, I kinda figured that out already. So, why are you here? And why do you want Harry and me here . . . with you?"

I folded the corner of the book page and carefully set it on the scarred coffee table before me. Lust had died before the grief. I didn't want to see Harry's regret or Lori's sympathy, so I closed my eyes, slid down, and rested my head on the back of the couch. The story of Eileen's death, the description of my helplessness, and the explanation of my move to the slums poured out. I had a killer to find who was linked to the convenience store robberies around town. Harry had said word on the street was the robberies originated from the slums. He volunteered to help me find my way around until I picked up the killer's trail.

Their silence got to me. Finally, I opened my eyes. No regret in Harry's eyes, just determination and a touch of pride. Lori gripped the seat of her chair and I watched her swinging feet like a little girl trying to think up something to say.

"You have a problem believing that . . . or what?"

"No." She chewed her lip. "You must have a lot of money, like Harry said."

"I have enough to live on . . . for a while . . . long enough. Why?"

"You said Harry is helping you. I don't know if you're paying him . . . but, if you want to give me part of the action, like a job, I can help you find this man."

"How?"

"Bob!" She obviously didn't like explaining herself and worked not to sound like she was apologizing or begging. "I'm a goddamn whore. I've seen more hanging johns in the past ten years than you have in the boy's locker room at your goddamn school. If he's here abouts, I probably went to bed with the guy you want."

Leaning forward I rested my chin in my hand and studied her. "You may be right. You might be able to find him. But you would have to go back to street walking. I could act as your pimp to be on the scene, but it would all be a front. You wouldn't really do any more tricks. We'll make everybody think I'm your man. That should keep Fox and any others away from you. And while you are making your rounds, you could look at the men and collect information. Yeah, it could work."

"Bob, Bob, Bob, you're losing it!" Harry stood up and paced to the door and back. "Think about what you just planned out! Nobody on the streets knows you. It's a war zone out there, not the halls of some high school or a TV show. These dudes pull real guns, just like Alabama did."

My thoughts flew. This was going to work. I could feel it. "Okay. You and Lori pass the word around that I'm a tough guy from Chicago, a real bad ass. Tell them no one wants to mess with me."

"That ain't gonna work!" Harry groaned. "Words are nothing! You gotta prove yourself. Get a gun. Flash it." His face changed, hardened. "But you better be damn ready to use it if trouble comes calling. You wanna go that far? This is dangerous stuff. Before you know it, the cops and the bad guys will be checking you over, maybe working you over. Is that what you want?"

"If that's what it takes to get Eileen's killer . . . then yes. I don't care, Harry. Can you get me that gun or not?"

He blew out a long breath. "Yeah, I know some people."

"Good. Let's get started." I looked at Lori as she stood, adjusting her towel and looking expectant. "You have anything else to say?"

She gave me a lop-sided smile. "Yeah. You are one dumb son-of-a-bitch. You don't want a whore, but you'll front one, all to get yourself dead. 'Cause that's what you'll be in less than two months. But if you find what you're after, you don't care. I gotta respect that and I don't respect much." She pushed a strand of drying hair behind her ear. "I like the feeling, especially if I can help. But . . . if I'm not whoring, I need money coming in. So, how much are you paying me?"

"How about a thousand a month, plus room and board?"

"Really?" Her genuine smile could have lit the entire block until Christmas. "But in cash with no damn IRS."

"It's a deal."

"If she's getting a thousand, am I getting that much over my Stop-and-Go salary? Maybe I shouldn't be working there at all. What can you front for me? Think I could make it as a male prostitute?" Harry's sarcasm wasn't missed.

"Go to the court house then get my damn gun!"

Chapter Six

A spring breeze lifted Eileen's hair, its strands separating and floating like silk threads. I wanted to touch that hair, so I would know how to paint it on canvas some day. My fingers just wouldn't let go of the fishing rod. Something pounded against the side of the wooden boat, jarring my concentration. The murky water sloshed about us. Eileen hadn't moved. She just stared, waiting for me to reach out. The pounding came again.

My eyes opened. Through the apartment window, morning light reflected off the brick wall across the alley. I rolled over, balling up the fresh-out-of-the-package sheets covering my new mattress. Three days ago I laid out four thousand dollars for new furniture, but had forgotten to buy curtains to block out the goddamn sun.

A fist hammered wood. "Open up!" a deep man's voice shouted. "This is the police!"

I shoved my legs into my jeans, tripped over the bare canvases stacked beside the bed, and stumbled out the bedroom door. "I'm coming!" I shouted back.

The 9mm Beretta Harry had found for me lay on the polished oak dining room table, in plain view of the front door. He had told me not to ask where it came from. While cleaning it, I had pulled the slide back and, of course, found the serial numbers filed off. Another impatient knock. I scooped up the weapon and shoved it under the deep cushions of the new couch on my way to the door.

The peep hole's distorted image showed one man waiting in the hall, the police detective, Sergeant Morten. I opened the door. He looked me over, his expression professionally cold.

"Morning, Sergeant Morten. What brings you here?"

He warily cocked his head. "I'm, ah, investigating a homicide and need to ask you some questions."

"Is it about my wife? Have you found her killer?"

He blinked then his face relaxed in recognition. "Bob Norris, isn't it? No, ah, we haven't found a suspect in that case . . . I'm surprised to find you . . . here. This is . . . about one Humphrey Jackson, known on the streets as Alabama. I was told I would find a Harry Piston living here."

His crisp tone irritated the hell out of me. "Yeah, Harry lives here and so do I. I don't know if he's home yet. You got me up! What time is it anyway?"

"Six thirty. Piston left work at the Stop-and-Go an hour ago. Shouldn't he be home by now?"

"Wait a minute, Morten. I don't care if you are a cop. You wake me out of a sound sleep and demand I tell you somebody else's business?"

He pushed his face toward me. "My job, Norris, is to make demands."

"Okay, asshole, have it your way." His arrogance was making my street attitude more natural. I'm actually enjoying this. "I didn't hear him come in, but I'll check."

He stepped forward with "And I'll come in while you do that."

My raised hand stopped him. "Not unless you have a warrant or I invite you. And I'm not inviting!"

At the end of the hall, the elevator rumbled to a stop. The doors opened and Harry stepped out, his arm wrapped around a grocery bag.

"Hm, I guess, he's home now, isn't he?" I snapped.

Morten gritted his teeth at my sarcasm. Harry only glanced at him as he walked around us. I took the bag.

"We have a visitor, Harry. Remember Sergeant Morten?"

He stared at the man for a long moment. "Been two weeks, but how can you forget a careful man like him."

"Mr. Piston, I have some questions and want you to come downtown with me."

"You can't question me here?"

"No."

"Is this about Eileen Norris?"

"No, it's another matter."

"Hey, Sarge, I'm tired. I worked all night. You can ask your questions here or get a warrant."

Morten expelled a long breath, rubbed his neck, then tried a friendlier expression. "Okay. Here. So, Norris, are you going to invite me inside now?"

"Come right in." I grabbed Harry's arm and practically dragged him to the couch. "You sit here, Harry. Get comfortable," I said pointedly. He glanced at the now-empty table and settled himself. Morten took the armchair across from him.

"I need coffee. Want some?"

Harry nodded.

"Offering any to the asshole?" Morten asked.

"Why not?" I threw over my shoulder as I headed to the kitchen with the groceries. Trying to be as quiet as possible, I listened to the living room conversation.

"Mr. Piston, we talked to someone who recognized you coming into this building four days ago, the morning of Wednesday the 19th. An hour prior to your arrival a pimp known as Alabama entered this same building with a street whore named Lori Saint. This witness works across the street at the Laundromat. She did not see you or Alabama come out. Now, do you know Alabama?"

I held my breath, my heart rate accelerating.

"I've seen him around. I wouldn't call us exactly friends."

"Did you see him in this apartment building?"

"No. Bob and I just moved here. I go to work, come home, go to bed. Haven't seen too many people period."

"Exactly when did you move in?"

"Four days ago."

"You and Bob Norris . . . together."

"Right. He's the one paying the rent. We been friends for a few years. He wanted a change after . . . well, you know. And he wanted company, so he offered me one of the bedrooms."

"Sounds like things are going your way . . . kind of sudden like. Nice place to live. Fancy new car. Did you buy that with the money you took off Alabama . . . after killing him?"

I erupted from the kitchen yelling "What the hell are you talking about? I bought that car! Me, the rich guy! Put it in his name! Harry didn't kill anybody! Why don't you get your pig ass out of here!"

Morten rose to his feet, coldly assessing my anger. "Norris, what is it about you that rubs me wrong? Even at your wife's murder scene, you acted like a jerk toward me. Why is that?"

Memories of the Chicago peace march down State Street flashed across my mind. I shivered, recalling the cops with their tear gas and night sticks. "You goddamn cops are all alike. Beat down innocent people and call it your job. I was in a peace demonstration in the '60's. Peace! Ha! Your brother cops burned us with tear gas and broke our faces with night sticks. And peaceful citizens are supposed to trust pigs like you? Trust you to do your job? That's a laugh! Your job is to find Eileen's murderer, and you haven't done a damn thing, have you?"

"Back off, Norris. We're investigating. You get clear on this: that homicide is not the only one in this city. I am here investigating another one. You want to stick your nose in, then you answer some questions, too. Why are you living here?"

"Couldn't deal with an empty house. I needed a change for a while . . . just like Harry said. Now, you tell me if my living here has one goddamn thing to do with your homicide investigation!"

"Alabama and his whore lived across the hall from you! How's that for close enough? Did you know him?"

"We were never introduced." That's the truth, anyway!

"How many days ago did you and your friend move in?"

"Four!"

"And that's the day in question. How's that for another coincidence, Norris? Did you hear anything suspicious in the building?"

"Like what?"

"Like a gunshot, Mr. Peace Demonstrator. Alabama was shot to death. He was seen coming into the building, but not leaving. Maybe he was killed here."

"And you think Harry shot him?"

"Piston came home, then the pimp ended up dead."

"Do you have proof Harry killed our supposed neighbor?"

"No, not . . . yet. So, we'll move on. Either you know Alabama's girl, this Lori Saint . . . or the whore's whereabouts? I have a warrant for her arrest."

"Morten, your little visit has been a waste of time, yours and ours. I don't know any whores. Do you, Harry?"

Harry twitched a rueful smile. "I've known one or two. And I seen this Lori in the Stop-and-Go, but not in the past few days. You trying to arrest anybody and everybody for killing her pimp?"

The sergeant shook his head slowly and started toward the door. "The warrant was issued before Alabama died . . . by her parole officer. If she comes to that door across the way, tell her to give him a call." He turned to look each of us in the eye. "I'll be watching you two. If you hear anything or have anything interesting to tell me about Alabama, call the station."

We waited for the elevator noise to fade before either of us moved. Harry stood, stretched, then dropped into the chair Morten had abandoned. He nonchalantly picked up the TV remote, thumbed the volume up, and shifted his attention to me.

"What now?"

I lifted the cushion and palmed the Beretta. "I don't know. He said he would be watching us. You're the street-smart one here. Does that mean he's on to us?"

"Naw, he's just snooping and an asshole."

"That's real news! Who's the witness that works in that laundramat? I've never seen anybody over there."

"Bet it was Candi."

"Who?"

"One of Fox's girls. She doesn't work in the Laundromat. She works in front of it. You think she's going to tell the cops that? Anyway, I remember seeing her when I came home that morning."

A headache crawled around inside my skull. For three days Harry and Lori had been filling my head with information about the habits of the area's whores, gangsters, petty criminals, and the newer gang elements. I felt like I had been studying for some kind of final exam. "I'm trying to fit in here and I piss off a cop . . . who is investigating what I don't want him to and goddamn ignoring what he should be doing!"

Harry grinned at me. "But you're doing his work for him, right?"

My head throbbed. I envisioned an apartment out by Lake Crazy Horse with straight-laced, safe Maggie living across the hall from me, and the ghost of a sleazy pimp. Shoving the gun back under the couch seat, I rubbed my stomach. "Who gives a damn if he's watching us! You want to take a drive for breakfast?"

"Don't think so. I grabbed fast food on my way from the store. Oh, yeah . . . I noticed your new car in the garage. Not exactly a pickup truck!"

"Lori thought a sporty car looked more like something a pimp would drive."

"You think it will bury my Mustang?"

"I think I'm not interested in dragging. I'm interested in breakfast. Morten can watch me eat. See you when you wake up."

"Yeah. Later," the disappointed Harry mumbled, scooting down in his seat to stare at the TV.

Cabinet doors slammed in the kitchen. I found Lori leaning against the counter, pulling the pot from the coffee maker. A football jersey hung to mid-thigh. Her mussed hair and sleepy expression gave her back her teen years. That would make a nice image on canvas.

"Your coffee's ready. Want some?"

"Forgot about it." I took the mug from her. "What time did you get in?"

"Early. Around two."

"We woke you, huh?"

"All cops are assholes. You got that part right."

"Harry said Morten was fishing. First about him then about you. Did you hear the warrant part . . . from your parole officer?"

"I think that's why I didn't show my face, hayseed!"

"Of course," I mumbled, duly chastised.

We sipped our coffee. I tried not to look at her shapely legs as she leaned back against the counter and crossed her feet at the ankle.

"Did you do any business last night?"

"Johns? I ain't got a street to work on. Remember? I sat in an all night diner. But . . ." she smiled triumphantly before continuing,

"Fox showed after midnight."

"Perfect! What did he say?"

"That he wants to kill you." She ignored my coughing as I swallowed wrong. "By now everyone on the streets knows you as 'Picasso.' Harry and I made you out as an educated bad ass from Chicago, like you said. We also put out the word that you killed Alabama. That's why Fox is pissed, of course."

"Good . . . I guess. This is all moving so fast. Hope nothing goes wrong. So, how soon is he coming after me?"

She shrugged. "Said he has to figure out a really bad pay back for dumping your trash on his turf. He's pretty hot, so I'd say soon. Are you ready?"

"Harry took me down by the river yesterday. I shot off about a 100 rounds. And we did a little work out. Like that martial arts crap, but just enough for me to dodge and roll. Harry's really good at it. You wouldn't expect it of him with just one, ah, I mean, all these years after Nam."

"You like him, don't you."

"He was there when Eileen . . . and now he's here. And it's not just the money. He's knows what needs doing."

"I didn't tell Fox where you live, but his girls will. I wouldn't do any walking around the area, even if you can dodge and roll real good."

I laughed, she didn't.

"Bob, this isn't playtime. This is real. You sure you want to go through with this?"

"Yes, Lori. I started this scenario and I'll finish it. I've gone too far. I feel like-like Eileen's depending on me."

For the first time since I met her, her eyes glistened with rising tears. She turned to set her cup in the sink.

"What's the matter?"

"Just leave me alone," she whispered.

When she didn't move or even look up, I got the message and returned to the living room. Harry slept in the chair, the TV hummed an unnoticed noise in front of him. He hadn't been in the kitchen, so he hadn't taken his morning pills waiting in two brown plastic bottles on the counter.

For some reason Lori had assumed the job of reminding him every morning and every night. She announced she only did it to keep him from flipping out around her. He accused her of taking up nursing to harass men, since she'd given up whoring. His "Nancy Nurse" name-calling made us all smile.

Because Lori had slipped back to her bedroom, it would be my turn this time. I read the labels carefully before taking one capsule from each bottle. For a moment I stared at the VA Hospital markings on the bottles. How simple for them to shove a few pills at men like Harry and forget further responsibility for their condition. And if fascist politicians had only paid attention to peace demonstrations like mine, they wouldn't have committed the crime of sending whole boys into war to become men with twisted minds and bodies. Men like Harry who needed VA Hospitals. Men who needed dignity . . . not pills.

I set the glass of water on the table and bent over the sleeping man. First, I nudged him and softly called his name. When he merely shifted restlessly and rolled his head, I grabbed his shoulder and shook him harder.

A grinding roar through clenched teeth startled me. His arm locked around my neck. My breath whooshed out as Harry pinned me against his chest.

"Harry!" I gurgled. "It's Bob! Bob! Let . . . go!"

My twisting and thumping overturned the table. Still he held me. The menacing roar rumbled from his chest, but the sound began to fade as my sight darkened. The pressure around my neck eased, the roaring turned to groans, and I slid to the floor at Harry's feet. Gulping in air, I realized Lori stood behind the chair, her palms massaging Harry's temples, her voice whispering soothing nonsense words in his ear. His whole body relaxed. He tried to open his eyes, but they rolled as if he was dizzy and trying to stop the spinning inside his head.

"Th-Thanks," I managed as I stood up. "There's his goddamn pills."

By the time she got him to swallow them, Harry was leaning forward and rubbing his own head, still not able to communicate. It was then I noticed Lori's red and swollen eyes.

"Why were you crying?"

"You son-of-a-bitch! Do you really think you can kill Fox? You can't even protect yourself from-from a friend!"

"Kill Fox? I wasn't thinking of killing him. I was thinking of scaring him, maybe shooting him in the leg . . . if I had to."

"You stupid bastard! He wants to . . . kill . . . you." She enunciated like I was a simpleton. "Scare him? You don't kill him first . . . you will be as dead as . . . as your wife. Is that what you want? What you really want?"

God! Was it? "No," I whispered, then shouted "No! I never thought of it that way."

"How can I make you understand? You're out of time. No more of this target practice or talking bullshit. You either quit now . . . or you kill him!"

Tears welled up again. She swiped at them.

"You were crying over me?"

A sigh escaped from Harry. Lori sat on the arm of his chair, one hand rubbing his back, the other tugging at the hem of her jersey.

"Did I, ah, miss something?"

"Yeah, your goddamn pills," I said.

"I didn't hurt anything, did I?"

"You tried. You just about did Fox's work for him."

"Fox? What?"

"Lori here seems to think Fox means to come after me."

"Man, I did miss something. That's what we want, isn't it?"

"I told him Fox means to kill him."

"So? That's why I'm here."

Lori and I exchanged glances. "Okay, Harry, but for a little added insurance, I'm running to Electronic City for a few things. Get some sleep. Lori, put on those jeans of yours, because you are coming with me."

Chapter Seven

A block from Electronic City, I eased the Ferrari into a parking space. Lori got out and stepped to the sidewalk. I fumbled with the car manual, trying to avoid looking at her petite figure clad in the loose print sun dress, instead of the jeans I had dictated. Her light touch of make-up over that creamy complexion . . . the image began to mentally transfer to the bare canvas propped on the easel in my room. I scowled at the manual's section marked "Car Alarm."

"Hey, Bob! You coming or not?"

My door slammed a little harder than I intended. "Hold your pants on . . ." Wrong, stupid! "I mean, just a minute." My thumb pressed buttons on the remote, while I listened to her nervous pacing. Through the tinted window I saw the red light blinking. With a triumphant smile I finally joined her. "With any new piece of equipment, Lori, there is a learning curve—"

She grabbed my arm. "There's Worm!"

I looked down, but found my fly zipped. "What are you talking about?"

"There, down the street I told you about him. He watches out front, while someone else breaks in. If cops come by, he signals."

I tried to nonchalantly glance where she indicated. "You think he's on a job now?"

"Here he comes. Act natural!"

How the hell was someone suppose to act natural around a criminal? I took her arm and pretended to be looking for an address. Two steps later a slender boy blocked our path. He looked like many belligerent teens I had known over the years, only harder, more vicious. His ankle-length trench coat was obviously too heavy for summer and reeked of sweat.

I didn't look away from his stare. "Is this kid looking for trouble?" I asked Lori.

"Don't ask me. Ask him."

"I thought I just did."

He jabbed me in the chest with one finger, "Are you

Picasso?"

I blinked then remembered. "Yes, I am. Why do you ask?"

"We been on the lookout for you . . . for Fox. He's down the street . . . doin' business, if you know what I mean."

When I glanced at Lori, she shrugged, not taking her eyes off the pimple-faced kid. "Well, we got business, Worm."

"You know, bitch, Fox don't like waitin'."

"Then you run and tell him—"

"Yo, whore! You don't get it!" His bad breath spewed in her face as his hand flipped back the coat and settled on the butt of a gun shoved in the front of his jeans.

I had forgotten my own gun! Lori squeezed my arm as I tensed. "We're supposed to be impressed with that?" She asked. "It probably replaces somethin' you've never used!"

His lips curled in a snarl, as he jerked his head for me to walk in front of him.

"Have you ever thought about seeing a dermatologist or a dentist?" I asked. He stiffened, but his eyes flicked away this time. I loosened Lori's hold on my arm. "I'm going. You're not."

She pressed her lips to my ear as if kissing me. I shivered. "Go along with whatever Fox says. Don't get yourself killed. I'll bring Harry."

The gentle pat to her cheek and my wink only made her roll her eyes. She backed away aiming a cocked finger at Worm. He merely grunted and shoved me on my way. I stumbled. Spinning back in irritation I froze. The gun looked much bigger outside his pants. I lifted my hands in concession, thankful they weren't shaking. He concealed the gun in a fold of the coat, but I couldn't figure out why. The few passersby, either in cars or on foot, looked like the types to be carrying guns, too. Worm shadowed me close enough that I could feel an occasional nudge from the gun and smell him to boot. Mind's probably been replaced by ditch weed marijuana. I decided to follow his every command and not tempt him to use that gun.

Lori had accused me of planning to carefully. But 25 years of lesson planning and weaving my life around Eileen's to avoid her father as much as possible . . . I was a planner by habit, dammit! Some of Harry's practice moves ran through my mind, immediately followed by an image of Chuck Norris. I'm simply Bob Norris, for crissakes! The Norris who knows nothing and wants to stay alive long enough to learn . . . something!

My swinging hand brushed the Ferrari keys in my pocket. I almost groaned remembering Lori said she was going for Harry. Yeah, on foot! That could take more minutes than I could afford. And what the hell could Harry do, a one-armed Chuck Norris..Yeah, right! I got Lori and Harry into this with me. It's time for me get this over with . . . so I can get back to the hunt. The hunt. That sounded right!

Sweat trickled down my face and soaked into my T-shirt the "Nine Nails" sticking to my body. At the corner of 10th and Howard, Worm shoved me one last time, toward a black Lincoln. He hadn't noticed my sweat.

The Lincoln's back door opened. I leaned over to enter and peered down a double barrel shotgun. A deep, rasping voice came from the tinted window, shadowed interior, "Have a seat and no funny stuff!"

"I don't see any humor in this, anyway," I quipped stepping in and dropping back into a lush seat.

The door slammed shut and the interior darkened even more. I could feel the man with me. His aftershave smelled clean and expensive.

"So you . . . are Picasso?"

"Yeah, that's what some call me."

"Tough, eh? From Chicago? Why is it nobody up there knows you?"

"I don't make many friends."

"I want some straight answers, punk. I want them now! Who took out Alabama?"

"I did."

"Quit wasting my time or I'll pull the damn trigger on the piece I'm aiming at your pecker."

My insides began to quiver, but my hands rested quietly on my knees. "You don't want to do that, Mr. Fox . . . or is it just Fox?"

"Fox. Talk, mister!"

I took a deep breath smelling my own nervous sweat and his clean scent. "Well, Fox, I am serious. I did have a part in 'taking him down.' In fact that's a very accurate idiom, ah, term. I hit him on the back of the head with a chair and his gun went off as he fell . . . killing him, taking him out, taking him down, whatever."

The ensuing silence tortured my nerves. My eyes adjusted to the dimness. The broad-shouldered man filling the opposite corner of the back seat sat still, his eyes narrow, the end of his shotgun big. The barrel lifted from pointing to my crotch to the center of my chest. I couldn't swallow.

"I've been wanting to kill that son-of-a-bitch for two years . . . and he shoots himself . . . on accident?" He chuckled, a guttural, mean attempt at humor. "So, Picasso, what did you do with his money? Wait! Lori took at least her three thousand. But Alabama always carried ten grand. Where's the rest?"

I raised both hands carefully. "I swear I did not take any money. It was shoved into one of his pockets . . . well, after Lori took what she was owed, but . . . how did you know she did that?"

"It's my business to know my girls, the way they think. And she is gonna be one of mine."

"Oh, you don't want her. You're a man of quality. I know you don't want her."

"Is that so? Did you decide to pimp her?"

"Hardly! I-I took her to bed the other night, after Alabama's . . . Anyway, she had these big sores and smelled like sardines, that sweet-sore—"

The gun moved forward. "Are you giving me more shit?"

At least my uncomfortable laughed sounded authentic. "Why would I lie about a whore? We're both businessmen. I wouldn't want my clients contaminated. Neither would you. Right?"

My gaze flicked from the gun to his expression. I couldn't tell much in the poor lighting. Then the gun drooped and he relaxed.

"Since the apple's spoiled, what are you going to do with it?"

"She's got potential. Nice to look at. My pockets are deep. She'll have medical bills, hospital and all. When she gets well . . .

I'll collect from her . . . then call you."

The gun disappeared inside the big man's coat. "Naw. That's all right. You keep her. You know, while you talked I began to think we've met before."

My butt settled more comfortably into the seat, but I gauged my hand grabbing the door handle and the roll out the door . . . if it became necessary. "Well, Fox, I don't think so. I'm new to town—"

"Three years ago!" he interrupted, leaning forward, his expression bright, almost friendly. "My son went to East High. You teach art there! Met you at a parent-teacher thing!"

"Ah, you have a son?"

"Sent him off to college in New York. Fucking expensive, but he's doing great!"

My insides began to fold inward. This was not part of the plan. Thoughts ricocheted around my brain. "Ah, what's his name?"

"Doesn't matter. You are that Norris, right?"

"Yeah. I mean, yes, I am."

"Always liked you. You helped my boy. He talked about you more than any other teacher. I guess that's why he's studying that fucking art shit now. And he's good. Well, his grades are good. You got him started. I want to do you a favor. Name it."

"Oh, no . . . no, sir, ah, Fox . . . Wait. Yes, maybe you can do me a favor." Within twenty minutes, I had everything explained from Eileen's shooting up to Morten harassing us over Alabama's death. "I'm looking for my wife's killer because the police aren't."

"Lori's idea to plant Alabama in my alley, huh? Joke's on me. Guess I'll owe her one. And you said it was Morten who came about his dead body? That explains where the seven thousand went!"

"He took it?" I yelped in surprise.

"Sure! He's pulled money off my girls and kept it. Why wouldn't he steal from the dead?" A dark laugh rumbled from his chest. "But, someday, I'll get it from him, every last dollar."

"Why is this money so important?"

"It's called a kitty. If you are going to be on the streets, Norris, you listen up. Once somebody gets knocked off, a respectable street person, like myself, will take the kitty and pass it on to the widow . . . if he has one, or to a family member. Alabama had a wife and two kids. Now, I gotta take that money out of my own pocket . . . so they don't suffer. Do you see?"

"Kinda. But you were . . . like rivals."

"Listen and learn, Norris. This was lesson one. We take care of our own. Now, get out of here, 'cause I gotta talk to some of my people. I'll be in touch."

My hand froze on the door handle. Movie images of people shot in the back played across my mind. "So . . . this means you are not going to kill me."

"We pay our debts on the street, Norris. You helped my son become what he is today. That saved your ass from getting real dead, but . . ." He slapped my knee. "I was after Alabama anyway and Lori ain't worth much to me, sick or not . . . so I still owe you for my son. Here on out, you stay out of my business and you'll be okay."

As I stepped onto the sidewalk, the Lincoln squealed into a traffic lane and swung around a corner. A huge sigh released my tension. I backtracked to my car, taking long, determined strides. Half a block from the Ferrari, I thumbed the remote to shut down the alarm and unlock the car. It's alarms squealed instead. Glancing around I saw three people stop to eye me. I punched the remote until everything fell silent and the door opened. I backed out of the parking space and laid some rubber of my own. Fox had his business and I had mine!

At the apartment I found Lori huddled on the sofa, a tissue pressed to her nose. She threw her arms around my neck, that tight little body slamming against mine as she hysterically cried, "Bob! Oh, Bob! You're back!"

"Of course." I tried to disentangle those arms, before I embarrassed myself. "You're crying again. Are you pregnant or something?"

"So . . . so is he dead?"

"No! Why were you so damned worried. Fox is a nice guy. I didn't get to see much of him, inside his dark car, but we had a really pleasant talk."

"Pleasant? Fox? Are you kiddin' me? Fox doesn't give anyone a break. He put out the word he was gonna kill you!"

"Not anymore. We talked. Now he's gonna help me find Eileen's killer."

"You talked him into that? Bull! You took down Alabama and you took Alabama's territory and me—"

"He's not interested in you anymore. He's not going to bother you for a long time. I told him you have bad case of herpes."

"God dammit-to-hell-and-gone! What the hell did you do that for? I won't be able to work the streets again? Did you think of that?"

"So what? Take up another profession, something a . . . ah, you know, a—"

"You are trying to say 'Something a nice girl would do,' aren't you? Listen, stupid! Once a whore, always a whore. Whores work for pimps or get thrown through the county ER doors beat up and near dead. No pimp is going to put an infected whore on the street. So you just put me out of work. Period."

"Now, you listen to me, Lori!" I was tired of being lectured to like I was the child here. "Someday you will thank me for this. And you are not out of work! You are helping me investigate a murder."

"How? Sitting in this cramped apartment with all your new shit, watching TV, counting the bricks on the wall across the street—"

"Lori!" I shouted. "Shut up! Where's Harry?"

"Out looking for you!"

"His Mustang is still in the garage."

She folded her arms across her chest. "You're getting so street smart, you figure out why."

I rubbed my face and focused on controlling my temper. Here was a young woman who knew how to push the right buttons. She had done it to Alabama and now she was working me in retaliation for my butting into her business. "Okay, Miss Smart Alec, he's out walking the streets. That means he's talking to people, people he knows, his connections. They aren't the most trust-worthy types, so . . . he left the car home so it wouldn't get stolen behind his back."

"And whose the Smart Alec?"

"So, I'll ask your advice. Do I wait here or go looking for him?"

She rolled her eyes and sighed heavily. "The phone man came right after we left. Harry said he'd call me every hour on the hour."

"Where—"

"Where do you think a phone should be, Mr. Smart-talking-man-who-don't-know-dick?"

I stared into her eyes for a long moment. Tears welled up again. She signaled with thumb over her shoulder toward the desk that filled the breakfast nook. As I turned back to apologize, she pushed past me and dropped on the couch.

Realizing I was going to be ignored, I examined the combination phone and answering machine Harry had ordered. For not having too much money, the man knew how to select quality. I scanned the instruction book open beside state-of-the-art equipment. Pushing the appropriate button, I listened to the crisp, nondescript greeting Harry had recorded.

"Harry should have been a secretary," I said. Lori continued to ignore me. She concentrated on the mirror and cosmetics spread on the table at her knees. With practiced strokes, she wiped away the evidence of tears and applied the barest suggestion of color to a face so different from the one I had first seen so few days ago. That face had looked hard, artificial, exaggerated, right down to the thick blonde wig that had disappeared.

I walked to the window to get another perspective of the indirect sunlight washing across her freshness. As my mind created another memory to be transferred to canvas, I stumbled over the decorative floor vase. It crashed over, spilling the dried flowers and country weeds across the wooden floor.

"Harry and I said you bought too much crap for this place!"

"Touches like this make it a home, not just a place."

"If you can move around and not break something."

The side of my foot worked well enough to push the pottery shards and crumbling foliage against the baseboard and out of my line of travel. When I finally got back to studying Lori, she had leaned back staring off into space, her hands unconsciously rubbing up and down her thighs.

"Have you ever had herpes, Lori?"

"You told Fox I did."

"Only so he'd leave you alone. But, I know diseases like that . . . How do you keep from getting them?"

"I make . . . made my johns wear rubbers. I still got gonorrhea last year. Treated it right away and I've been clean since."

"Then you see a doctor regularly."

"Not since that penicillin prescription."

"Won't do. Since you're my employee now, it's my responsibility to see you get a complete physical. I told Fox I had to take you to the doctor, so this will look good. I'll get an appointment with my doctor tomorrow."

"The clinic has always been good enough."

"Not anymore. Now you'll see Dr. Burroughs. My wife and I have seen her for years."

"Her? A woman doctor?"

"Are you prejudiced? She has a very good reputation—"

"I can't believe you see a woman doctor, not unless she's good looking."

I thought a moment. "I suppose she is, but that has nothing—"

The phone's ring saved me from digging the hole Lori expected. Dr. Burroughs is damn good looking and I'm not her only male patient. I glanced at my watch to stop my thoughts. "Hello, Harry. Where the hell are you?"

"So you finally showed up . . . alive! I been dragging my tired ass all over looking for you, or your dead body."

"Appreciate it. I'm fine. Fox is letting me live. Actually he's doing better than that. Where are you at? I can pick you up."

"Stay put. I'm going to drop on this here bus bench and get some sleep. Between the phone company, a chauffeur named Charles, and that damn Lori . . . I didn't get more than twenty minutes of sleep today."

"Charles? Harry! Did you say Charles? When did you see him?"

"He came to the door after the phone man left. He said

something about your father-in-law. I put the message on the refrigerator with those fancy candy magnets you bought. It says the old man wants to see you as soon as possible."

Chapter Eight

Against the far wall, the repulsive bastard sat in a high backed chair behind a large oval table. A pure white cloth starkly contrasted the red china place settings, two of them. Amato's offered the city's finest dining experience. And here, lowly Bob Norris had been invited into Amato's private dining room. Of course, I was to feel honored and aware that what Henry was about to say was immensely important.

The ever proper Charles escorted me across the elegant room. I had to bite my tongue to keep from saying "Thanks, Chucky." The man didn't deserve my annoyance. He pointed to the seat and table setting to the right of my father-in-law. I took the chair to the left.

Henry stared at me for a moment. "You are excused, Charles." A sip of water. "Well, hello . . . Robert. I am glad you came on such short notice . . . and that you chose to wear the DaVinci I had tailored for you last year."

"My polyester's at the cleaners. Since finding the message on my frig yesterday, I had plenty of time to shave and brush my teeth . . . repeatedly."

"Everything is a big joke to you, isn't it? Please have the courtesy to sit here where there is a plate."

"I prefer here. The waitress can give me a clean one . . . if I stay. Why did you . . . summons me, Henry?"

He draped a folded, dark red napkin across his lap as the stoic young waitress poured his wine. One flick of his finger and she arranged china and utensils for me. No one spoke as the plates of salad were set down and aromatic Italian oil drizzled over the crisp lettuce. I merely stared at mine. Henry crunched away on his, slowly as if savoring the abrasive sound and the flavors.

Pushing indolently back in my chair, I was about to repeat my question when Charles re-entered. He set a large envelope on the table to Henry's right. His hesitation caught my attention and I looked up into eyes so like Eileen's. Damn! I had never noticed. Even his mouth and lips smiled in the same self-contained arrogance as

Eileen, as if he knew something and dared me to find out what. The smile disappeared. He straightened in a military stance.

"Sir, the messenger arrived."

"Thank you, Charles. Tell him I will not need his services for the rest of the day."

Trying to ignore my impulsive thoughts, I began to pick at my salad. First the green pepper had to go, then the sour, yellowish peppers. I looked up just as Henry ate his.

He delicately placed the stem on the edge of the salad plate, then casually moved that hand to the envelope. One twist of his wrist and several eight by ten photos slid onto the white tablecloth. Photos of Lori. He distastefully slid them together and placed them beside my plate.

"Do you know her, Robert?"

"I think you know the answer."

"Can you explain why she is living with you?"

"Can you explain why you have pictures of her?"

"Not important at the moment."

"You've had your damn investigators checking up on me again, haven't you?"

"Long ago, I accepted the responsibility to watch over you. You did marry my daughter and began receiving a portion of my money through her. I am a careful investor. Now . . . quit avoiding my questions. Who is this girl to you?"

"I've been old enough to vote for a long time . . . and my business is none of your goddamn business."

"Don't be crude, Robert. Your wife has been dead a very short time. You move to a disreputable section of town and take a mistress. Not particularly admirable actions. I wish to remind you of the two million dollars I gave you and Eileen as a wedding present."

"Gave, not invested. I don't remember signing any agreements at the time."

"No time for any prenuptial, as I recall, and Eileen convinced me there would be no need. Who would have believed you would outlive her?"

"Cut the bullshit, Henry. Get to the point. What does Lori—" I waved my hand over the photos, "—have to do with two million bucks you think you threw away?"

He sat up straighter, his eyes cold and narrow. "You will get rid of that prostitute and your store clerk friend. I expect you to move back into your home and take up your normal responsibilities. If you don't do what I ask, Robert, this matter will be referred to my attorney. Mr. Winters has found a totally legal procedure to freeze your various bank accounts."

"Don't threaten me, you son-of-a-bitch! I'll have my accounts transferred the minute I walk out of here."

He continued eating the remains of his salad. "A temporary court order was filled this afternoon."

The asshole refused to look back at me. The waitress removed the salads. The waiter at her shoulder uncovered plates of chef-arranged beef and potatoes with parsley sprigs. Henry began to eat despite my burning stare.

Calm down. Slow the heart rate. Could he be bluffing? How could he touch that money? His name was never on those accounts. Could strangle the bastard, but he isn't worth jail. But Fox might get away with it.

I stabbed my fork into a succulent piece of pink and brown beef. "Why are you doing this, Henry?"

"I loved my daughter. I feel you are being disrespectful of her and her family . . . by your actions and associations. Just the other day, Donald agreed—"

"Stop right there! You talked to my brother?"

"We met at the funeral. I found him well-spoken and respectful, even reasonable. You really should be more like him, you know. Anyway . . . I flew to Chicago a few days ago. We met for dinner at a restaurant owned by a football coach . . . a friend of mine you wouldn't know, of course."

Now he looked at me, a glint of triumphant in his eyes that chilled my blood. "Donald and I agreed you have become not only irresponsible, but unstable. Eileen's death was . . . a shock to us all, but it is time to get yourself together, to get on with your life . . . as Eileen would have wanted. Donald said you wish to retire from teaching. I agreed it was about time. A perfect change would be for you to step into the advertising department of either Bison Insurance or Ashland Steel. As a controlling officer on both boards, I can give you the position you choose."

The antique clock on the fireplace mantle ticked. Henry's knife grated on his plate. I watched him precisely cut the meat, just like he was cutting my options.

Or is he? You haven't learned anything about him in all these years, Norris? He's addicted to negotiation and Eileen . . .

"I need time. What would time cost you? Six months. Give me six months to find Eileen's killer, then I'll do as you say."

"That's why you . . . you moved to the slums? No wonder Donald didn't want to elaborate! He insinuated you couldn't accept her murder. But you want to become comic book avenger? Ridiculous!"

"Lot of other people agree with my assessment of . . . what happened. I now have the kind of friends that can help."

"In six months."

"Yes.

"And if you find him, then what?"

"I don't know. I'll make up my mind when the time comes."

"Afterward . . . will you come to your senses?"

"Once again, I don't know. This is all my mind can handle right now. Didn't you say one time I'm just a hare-brained artist who can't focus? Now I have a focus."

"And damned smart, when you want to be . . . in Eileen's words." Hooked! "All right. If I hadn't learned to gamble and take risks in my younger years . . . Well, I wouldn't be sitting on all these boards and living in the house on the hill."

I twisted my spoon in the julienne green beans on my plate "Interesting . . . I thought you lived closer to the clouds in order to look down on the little people of your world."

"Bad joke, Robert, but I will have the last laugh. The more I think about it, the more it sounds like this is a sure bet. Either way I win. You find the killer, justice is served. You don't, you will be seated in my office in six months, complying with my wishes."

Never happen, Old Man!

"Okay, I will change the court order, however I will not allow you to spend from your savings or investment accounts. You will be allowed four thousand a month from your checking. Not a penny more. That means no more spending on automobiles."

"Only four thousand? I have two people depending on me. What about them?"

"Robert, Robert," he groaned. "Why do you want to keep a prostitute of that caliber, when you could hire a better class—"

"She's helping me, and not in bed. I got her off the streets . . . and am paying her a salary. She is getting me to the people who know the dirt going on in this city."

He sipped his wine, then sighed heavily. Obviously he wanted me out of his life. "Why must you complicate everything you do, Robert? I'll put her on my pay roll . . . until she finds another line of work. I'm sure five hundred a week is less than she made hooking, but I'll not pay her a penny more. I suppose you're paying the one-arm man, too?"

Let him think he's in control and he's putty. "I'm sure your investigators told you he has a job, but, yeah, he's working for me too, kind of between a body guard-trainer and my own version of an investigator. He's not too proud. I'm sure he would appreciate anything you wish to give him . . . like me, I suppose."

"Don't push me, Robert. I'll tolerate this six months. Then you'll move up in the world to a better class of associates."

"Don't count on it," I mumbled but ducked as I added "asshole." No sense in irritating the quiet predator! Eileen had trained me not to be a total fool around this man.

As I sipped my untouched wine, Henry tapped his water glass with a spoon. "Charles! Robert is ready to leave now."

I looked at my barely touched food. "I am?"

"I have a business meeting here in . . . ten minutes. I am having dessert served . . . to them."

I shrugged and couldn't resist a parting dig. "Enjoy their butt kissing, Henry."

* * *

Chucky expertly squeezed the limousine into the noon hour traffic. I tapped on the partition glass. It slid down and I leaned on folded arms.

"How old are you, Charles?"

"Sixty-two, sir."

"Hm, five years younger than good Ol' Henry."

"Yes, sir."

"And still young enough to have some fun."

"I beg your pardon, sir?"

"Henry will be at Amato's for at least two hours. That's his minimum for a business meeting, as I remember. How about having some fun for those two hours? You could pick up my friends, Lori and Henry, and we could all go to a bar."

"Oh no, sir. I'm on the clock. A driver is never allowed to drink on duty."

"So you take us to the bar and I'll spring for a can of pop. For old times sake?"

Thirty minutes later Chucky parked the limousine in front of the Tickled Pink Bar and Grill. Two blocks around the corner from the apartment. The three of us sat side-by-side on the back seat, waiting for Chucky to open the door.

First, Lori giggled.

"What?"

"Ever see that picture of the three monkeys sitting on a limb? One had his hands over his ears—"

"Hear no evil, see no evil, speak no evil!" Harry's laugh filled the car. "That ain't us! I was wondering what the hell everyone's going to say when they see us climbing out this. Last time they seen anything this big, the governor visited two years ago."

"Why was the governor in this part of town?"

"Gave a speech on his 'War on Crime.'"

Chucky held the door. We emerged.

Lori poked Harry in the ribs. "So, was the governor for or against crime?"

Even Chucky smiled at that one.

Inside, we found a table towards the back of the dim room. On the wall closest to us hung a picture of a mounted cowboy racing beside a stage coach team, shooting back pursuing Indians.

The waitress sauntered up. Her gaze lingered on Chucky in his pristine chauffeur's uniform, but she knew the rest of us. The thin, tired face made her look at least thirty-five. Lori had told me Pam was twenty-eight then warned me to quit guessing or asking people's ages. They didn't like being reminded. The age thing wasn't a big deal to me. I just found it interesting that she looked so good in those black short-shorts and knotted t-shirt. Only today, the bottom half of the shirt had been cut off revealing her slim mid-drift. Harry held her gaze a moment. I saw her wink before she looked at me.

"Hi, Bob. You want the usual?"

"No. Had too much of that a couple of nights back. Get us a pitcher of beer and some glasses."

Moments later she returned. After unloading her tray, she squinted at Lori. "Heard you got the super itch, girl."

Lori stiffened. "Keep it up, bitch, and you'll eat it!"

"Whoa, there! Just makin' conversation." She began to fill our glasses.

I squeezed Lori's arm before throwing money on Pam's tray. Lori gave me a dirty look and relaxed back in her chair. Her pout looked like many I had seen in my classrooms. Chucky, on the other hand, sat in his chair as straight up as a cigar store Indian. He even stared ahead as if afraid to look right or left at his surroundings.

Maybe I had made a mistake bringing him here . . . but he had information I wanted. I considered the four-inch heads on piss-colored liquid in front of us. Nothing like cheap beer to loosen a man's tongue.

"Hey, Charles. Take off the jacket and loosen your tie. Consider yourself on a break."

"I must insist, sir, that I am on duty. I cannot drink beer."

"I forgot. I'll have Pam bring you a Coke or Pepsi."

"I think not. I'll wait in the car. No employer would tolerate this behavior. And, Young Lady, if you put your hand there once more, I shall call the police."

Lori's laughter bubbled up. "Come on, Chucky, loosen up. Join the fun. Bob's paying. Look at it this way! You got free beer, friendly folk to talk to . . . and I'm available this afternoon."

Harry leaned against my shoulder to whisper "Why did you bring him here?"

"He's close to my father-in-law and I need some info. We need to loosen him up."

The next moment Harry waved his arm across the table, knocking over a full glass of beer . . . that immediately flowed onto Chucky's lap. The cigar-store Indian gasped.

"Goddamn it! Shit happens, Man, especially when I gotta put up with one arm. Sit right there, Charles. I'll get something from the bar to clean you up."

Lori fisted napkins and vigorously dabbed at his lap. Chucky shoved her hand away and jumped to his feet, his chair tipping over.

"Damn it! Miss, I want you to leave me alone. Mr. Norris, I am leaving. I must change my uniform and be at the restaurant in time to pick up my employer."

I decided to seize the opportunity, because it wasn't likely to come again. It didn't matter if I lied to get the information I needed. "Hold it, Charles. Before you go . . . I have to know something. Just days before-before Eileen died, she talked about . . . well, she said you had an affair with her mother." He stilled, his eyes boring into mine. "She said it had been years ago, something long forgotten by everyone, but . . . she meant to talk to you, without Henry knowing, of course. She's gone, so I feel I owe it—"

With all the dignity a beer-soaked man could maintain, he sat down. He picked up Lori's glass of beer. For a moment I thought he would throw it at me. Instead, he put it to his lips and drank. Carefully he set the empty glass down, wiped the foam from his upper lip with a fresh napkin, and tapped the rim of the glass. Lori refilled it. Two long droughts and it was empty again.

"Sir, I have no idea how Eileen heard of that, but it is certainly none of your business."

Norris, you are getting good at this investigating stuff! I didn't smile. "I agree and I'm really sorry for bringing it up. However, in the conversation, I promised Eileen, if she didn't get the opportunity, I would take you aside. After all, Henry tended to ignore me . . . but she didn't get her questions answered, did she? In a way, I'm her representative now. So, for Eileen, what is the truth?"

His third beer finished, he slumped back in the chair. "May I call you Bob?"

"By all means."

His tone softened, probably from the beer and unleashed memories. "Well, Bob, it wasn't an affair. It was deep, abiding love. When Eileen's mother died, my life ended, too. Veronica and I were devoted lovers, long before Eileen's existence. When my employer left on his many business trips, Ronnie and I went to a cabin in Wisconsin. That was 'our home.' My heart shriveled when she died of cancer six years ago. Is that what you wanted? Do you feel better knowing?"

My eyes burned, but I had to take that final step. "Are you Eileen's father?"

"Yes." He cocked his head and studied me. "I have been your true father-in-law all these years. Only Ronnie and I knew. Not even . . . Not even my employer knew." His gaze counted each of us. "And that will not go beyond this table."

Lori and Harry only nodded.

"You have my solemn word," I said with conviction. "But there is one more thing. It will wait until we get you cleaned up and back in service."

Gently, Lori took Chucky's arm. He stood, no longer offended by her touch but a little unsteady on his feet. She led him towards the door with Harry and I on their heels.

At the limo, she looked him over from head to toe. "We may get him cleaned up, but he'll never be sober enough to drive. I have an idea." She handed Chucky to us, fished in his pockets, and pulled out the keys. I couldn't tell if he enjoyed her manhandling or was trying to wiggle away from her.

Lori slid behind the wheel. Chucky threw himself against the front passenger door. We had no choice but to put him next to her. Only the seat belt and shoulder harness kept him from ousting her. She ignored his protests as she swung the monstrous vehicle into the street and around the corner. At first Harry and I were going to offer backseat advice, but soon decided it was safer to buckle up our own seat belts.

Lori pulled into two parallel parking spots. I was grateful they were on the corner, but didn't doubt for a minute she would have tried parking the thing anywhere she decided it would fit.

"Watch him," she pointed at the bleary-eyed Chucky. "I'll be right back."

The three of us clueless males watched her disappear into a uniform shop. I nervously noticed the police uniforms on display in the window. When I started to comment, I found Harry leaned over the seat adjusting Chucky's restraints. The brewery-smelling chauffeur had passed out.

Minutes later, Lori slid back into the car, dressed in a double-breasted chauffeur's uniform even more formal than Chucky's.

"What's going on?" I demanded.

"I'm a regular customer here. I've dressed as everything from a nun to a sailor. You know, to please my johns."

"No, I don't know and I don't want to know. You can't take Chucky's place. You can hardly steer this damn thing around a corner. Henry will be pissed if you show up. Not only will you get your ass fired, but Chucky's, too."

"What do you mean he'll fire me?"

She backed the limo and pulled into the street. A horn blasted behind us.

"I forgot. You are on his payroll and you're making a thousand more a month than I was paying you."

"You gotta tell me how you talked him into that one! Right now, you and Harry take care of Charles." She threw me a dirty look in the mirror. "And his name is Charles, not Chucky." She concentrated on moving through traffic, her words sounding more precise, her manner changing from friendly to formal. "I will become the best damn chauffeur Henry has ever had. He might end up giving me another raise."

Wonder if she changed personalities right along with her clothes for her johns?

"Give me Henry's address."

"Do you know where Amato's is at?"

"Well, well! Yeah. Never been there 'til now, that is. I will let you three out and just about make it on time, I think."

"Are you the same Lori who challenged the bar girl?"

"You're a funny man, Bob."

"So, what are you going to tell him about Chucky, ah, Charles?"

"He got sick. Is there a cell phone back there? I've seen that in the movies."

"Who do you want to call? Fox?"

"I'm not laughing. Call Henry and tell him Charles got sick and you found a replacement."

"Won't work. He knows you. He has pictures. Remember?"

"He'll have more than pictures by the time I'm finished with him."

That sounded like the Lori I knew. Harry and I smiled at one another.

Chapter Nine

How could anyone be so pickled on so few beers? As we struggled to get Chucky up two flights of stairs, I knew Harry was thinking the same thing. He kept cursing the "Out of Service" elevator. The tall, lanky chauffeur lost his balance with each step, until we were almost dragging him. His heavy breathing sounded like his lungs were full of boiling water.

"Oh, for crissakes!" Harry wheezed and stopped.

Our "passenger" slid from his hold. Unable to maintain the weight by myself, I eased Chucky onto the steps. Harry bent closer to him.

"What's the matter?"

"This is more than a beer problem, Bob. He's not breathing too good. And he's getting paler by the second. Shock. Yeah, maybe from his heart. Get your butt to our phone and call a rescue squad."

I designated Harry to ride with Chucky to the hospital, so I could notify Henry. As I climbed those stairs again, I wondered how much money he would take from my allowance for getting his chauffeur drunk enough to land in the hospital. Maybe I had caused more than a drunken stupor. The paramedics hadn't wasted any time once they stuck wires on his chest to check the poor guy's heart. How could someone have so many problems because of a few beers?

Finding the answering machine light blinking, I punched it as I hunted for Henry's cell phone number.

"I'm using the limo phone, Bob! Why in hell didn't you call Henry before I got here? He didn't recognize me like you thought he would. He almost called the cops on me! I finally got him to believe I'm Charles's niece, but he's still waiting to hear from you about how his precious driver got sick. So do it! Oh, he can be reached at his office at Ashland Steel. I feel like a friggin' secretary!"

Henry's real secretary answered in her prissy monotone. I smiled, thinking of how Lori could liven up that office.

"Well, Robert?" Henry's voice demanded. "Where is Charles?"

"Rescue squad took him to St. Matthews Hospital."

A moment of silence. Henry cleared his throat. "Is this another of your non-humorous jokes?"

"Afraid not. I talked him into a couple of beers—"

"Charles drinking?" he interrupted me.

"Just a beer or two."

"I've never known Charles to consume one drop of alcohol. And, he's been taking medication for pack pain! He wouldn't think of mixing alcohol with that! What did you do to make him take a drink?"

I was glad Henry couldn't see my grimace. "I did nothing, Henry! He downed the beers! I didn't pour them into him! Calm down. I wanted to inform you before I follow the squad to the hospital. Join me there, if you're so damned concerned! Goodbye!"

"Wait, wait, wait!" Henry ordered.

"What?"

"Do you know this girl driving my car for him? She claims to be his niece. I know for a fact he has no family in the area."

"No, I don't know her." Give up art for acting, Norris! "He called her before he passed out. She was there in minutes. Is there a problem?"

"I do not associate with anyone I have not had investigated, though . . ." —I heard the sigh— ". . . she is courteous and an excellent driver. I'll check her out . . . perhaps hire her until Charles can return to work. And, yes, Robert, I will see you at the hospital!" He slammed the phone down as if beating me to it this time.

I rubbed my hands over my face. My mind filled with visions of Henry, Lori, and Harry conversing in a hospital waiting room. A wave of nausea surprised me. I burped the cheap beer.

Pulling into the hospital's U-shaped drive I spotted Harry lounging on a stone bench. He slid into the Ferrari's passenger seat with and exhausted sigh.

"So Chucky's okay or what?"

"He's alive and doing better."

"Is Henry with him?"

"Yep. Just got here."

"And Lori?"

"Didn't see her, but don't worry. I talked to Chucky before Henry arrived. He appreciates Lori trying to save his job. We didn't know what she told Henry, so he's claiming a memory lapse."

"Well, Henry didn't recognize Lori, but he didn't believe the niece bit either. Seems Chucky doesn't have any close relatives." Why did that idea cause a distant ache inside me?

"Tough to keep the lies straight, ain't it!"

"Very funny! Henry told me Chucky was taking some medication. It obviously didn't mix well with the beer."

Harry grunted. "That and the fact the old guy's got a heart problem. The next time you take someone drinking, Bob, why don't you ask a few questions. You almost killed the guy!"

"Me? I didn't make him drink all those beers, one right after—"

"Hey! Just like Alabama, right?" Harry grinned at me.

"Go to hell!" I scowled, he laughed.

Finally, I spotted Henry's limousine in the Bus Loading Zone. Lori waved us over. Harry lowered his window. She leaned in, her eyes sparkling beneath the uniform cap's brim.

"Henry's on his way down. Charles is in Coronary Care at least overnight, maybe longer."

I nudged Harry. "Thought you said he was okay."

"He's in the hospital and alive, ain't he?"

"Shut up and listen," Lori snapped. "Henry's got some weird crap going on. All the way over, he had that glass down so he could ask me questions between phone calls. Tonight I have to take him to a real spooky place."

"He's siccing his investigators on you, just like he does to everyone else. You better get out of this before he catches on to you."

"No. I can lie through my teeth and Charles will help. I know it. No, I'll earn my money from you . . . or good Ol' Henry . . . or whatever. My fuckin' point is I said I would help you. He mentioned your name and Eileen to whoever he was talking to. I can't walk the street and talk to snitches, so I'll find out what your father-in-law is up to."

Harry glanced at me and shrugged. No wonder her eyes were lit up. She had found a purpose and was determined. I had unintentionally set her up. This was not good.

"I do not want any more accidents or dying because of me!"

"What the fuck are you talking about? I'll just be driving and listening . . . well, and I'll call you every once and a while. Does that make you feel better? How else am I going to earn my money?"

I groaned. "Be careful! Henry is one devious and powerful son-of-a-bitch!"

"I'm warned. Now, get outta here before he spots you!"

We stopped at the Tickled Pink before going home. The flame-grilled burgers weren't as greasy as Jake's, but the limp fries provided what we missed. After our second round of beer, Harry belched, patted his stomach, and headed toward the restrooms. Pam set another beer in front of me.

"Sorry. I don't think I need another," I spoke up.

"It's from the red neck at the bar."

Turning, I counted ten possible red neck biker-types. Not a one acknowledged me. Harry returned. He sat down with a frown.

"Hey, where's mine?"

I shrugged. "Pam said some guy at the bar bought me this one." He looked around. "That one?"

A tall, slender man about my age threaded his way around the tables. His dark hair showed a line or two of gray and hung straight down the back of his leather vest. His full beard covered the opened neck of the plaid shirt. He took the chair next to mine and stared at Harry.

I rapped my knuckles on the table. "Ah, do we know you?"

His light-colored eyes shifted to me. He waited a long intimidating moment. "I'm Roy. You Picasso?"

Use of my new street name meant this was street business. Harry shifted in his chair, as if ready to jump if I gave the word. I cocked my head at Roy. "Yeah. What's, ah, what's up?"

"Can we talk without your friend here?"

"What does a cop want with Picasso?"

I blinked. "A cop?" I asked Harry then turned. "You're a cop?"

The stranger's expression didn't change, his eyes didn't leave mine.

Harry leaned onto the table. "He's got a Desert Eagle holstered under his vest, left armpit. Bad guys can't afford guns like that, not even on the black market. So, I say he's a cop."

Roy still didn't look at Harry. "Very observant, friend. Now move your ass somewhere else. I need to talk to this man."

"I don't know you. Harry stays. So, talk."

"This is between you and me. I don't like audiences."

"Tough. Harry and I are a team. Got that? Whatever you've got to say, we'll both hear."

Pam stopped the conversation as she set down two more beers. When she left, Roy relaxed. "Your friend Harry's right. I'm a cop. I saw you talking to Fox."

"Are you following me?" I immediately thought of Henry.

"Only after you visited Fox. What's your connection with him and who are you? I haven't seen you working this area before."

"You must be deep undercover if you can't get my identity from your own people."

"You could say that."

"I have no connections with Fox. I talked and agreed to dinner sometime."

"Bullshit! That's not how Fox does business. And the word was out he had 'business' with you. So, who are you?"

"No, you tell me first why you want to know."

"I don't have time for games. I can make your life a bitch or rewarding. Your choice."

Harry smiled. He always smiled when he expected a fight. My armpits itched with collected sweat. Wishing for something stronger, I gulped the beer.

Harry's finger tapped the table in front of Roy. "Hey, mister! Me! You listen to me. Get away from us. If you don't, I'll go to that phone by the can and have a dozen uniforms crawling all over this place in minutes. I'll just tell 'em to look for a tall, long haired bastard with a big gun."

"Really." Roy hadn't even blinked at the threat. My sweat turned to bullet-sized beads. Bad analogy, Norris. "You seem calm, level-headed, Harry. On the other hand, Picasso here looks ready for a nervous breakdown. Why is that?"

"I got no idea what they teach you at cop school about this undercover crap, but in Vietnam, fighting gooks, we learned give a little info, get a little info. That means it's your turn to talk."

"Lost that arm in Nam?"

"No, trying to saving some stupid hero's life. There. Like I said, it's your turn."

"I don't have time for amateurs. I want to give a warning. Picasso, you are stepping onto dangerous turf. Fox will chew you up before you can even think what's happening. You need drugs, women? Find 'em somewhere else. Fox is on a short fuse. He'll kill you first, then take your money. Simple as that."

A bitter laugh rumbled from Harry. "You are so off base, man! What kind of a cop are you? Maybe just a stupid one!"

Roy's gaze shifted from me to Harry and back. I shivered. "So what was the visit about?"

I couldn't hide the sheepish expression. "Did you know Alabama?"

He nodded.

I spilled my guts.

"Fox believed you stole the kitty. So, if you didn't, who did?"

"Morten. Detective Sergeant Mor—"

"I know who he is!" Roy interrupted. "Look, Picasso—"

"Bob. That's my name, okay?"

He nodded. "Bob, it is very interesting how things twist and weave together. In my book, it happens because it was meant to be. The department has been sniffing after Morten a long time. Bad cops get real good at covering their tracks. Out of nowhere someone, a civilian, trips him up. Interesting."

"So, do you have to take me in for questioning?"

Roy laughed. "Hell no! I'll make a few calls. I'm undercover. I carry around a lot of baggage from informants. Think I would have each one hauled to the station? Speaking of calls . . ." He took a pen from his vest pocket and wrote on a napkin. "That's my cell phone. Call any time you might need a little help."

"Why-why, thanks."

He pointed a finger at Harry. "You watch over this guy. He doesn't have the street look."

Harry grunted. "Yeah, I know. He bought me a Mustang and a Ferrari for himself!"

Roy pinched his eyes shut as if blocking the image. "Bob, pay attention to Harry. And know this. I'll work through my informants for you. With some teamwork, we'll find Eileen's killer."

As he stood, the cop aimed a finger Harry. He returned the gesture. My mouth almost gaped when Roy pulled a roll of bills from his jeans pocket and peeled off a couple. Loud enough for the bar flies to hear, he announced, "You get me some really high grade shit by Saturday and I'll add a bonus to that."

Harry palmed the money. Roy sauntered toward the door, patting Pam on the butt as he passed.

"You believe him, Harry?"

"Yeah, I do."

"Why?"

"It's in the eyes, Bob. We'll see that man again."

The afternoon melted away in a haze of more cheap beer and Harry's never-ending lectures on surviving the streets. At closing, we guided ourselves back to the apartment by keeping the curb to our left. I vaguely remembered glancing at the Ferrari in the Tickled Pink parking lot, its alarm light winking at me. Ernie's All-Nite Donuts across the street always had at least one cop car in front. They'd hear the car's goddamn alarm if it went off.

The climb up our stairs sobered me a little and sickened Harry a lot. He pushed me out of the way in his rush to the bathroom. I was grateful he made it. Turning toward my room with its blessed bed, I saw the answering machine light.

A rewind whir later, I heard Maggie's frantic voice. "Mr. Norris, call me right away. I have important information. I found out why

Eileen was killed."

My beer-fuzzed brain couldn't recall her home phone, so I wasted time fumbling with my address book. Finally, I punched in the numbers, their accompanying tones piercing my ear drum. Two, five, ten rings. No answer and no machine pick-up.

Chapter Ten

After coating my stomach with some pink stuff, I stretched out on my bed and begged for sleep. Maggie's message would not leave me alone. Back in the living room I picked up the old paperback novel. Words drifted before my eyes, but images would not focus in my brain. Focus.

A freight train slammed into my thoughts. Maggie had finally broken into Eileen's computer file. Of course, she found something incriminating. The file was about Frank Harper, the bastard who might have committed insurance fraud . . . killed his own wife . . . to collect her insurance. And I had the real goddamn thing in my closet!

I dug through the cramped storage space, shoving aside clothes and waiting art supplies. Finally, I looked up and there was Maggie's box on the top shelf. Setting it next to the coffee table, I settled on the couch with anticipation pounding in my head.

One by one, I pulled out file folders and looked at them. Some were crammed with forms, lots of forms with tiny print, insurance bullshit. I did see the names Franklin Harper and Carol Harper. Those had to be the policies, the contracts between the company and the insureds, so their folders went in the bullshit pile. Then I opened a slender folder and stared at a computer print out, only it wasn't in plain and simple English any idiot could read. It was in code, some encrypted computer code. Eileen's neat handwriting along the margin gave me the shivers. Frank Harper. Harper. Check date. Numbers with a question mark. Harper in town, question mark. Harper. Numbers . . . again. At the top of the margin of the next series of prints, she had written Harper in big letters, like she was angry, then drew an arrow pointing down. Below the arrow, more numbers and exclamation points then dashes, more dashes and question marks. At the bottom of the page, she had hurriedly scribbled "Ask secretary to look for this" and more exclamation points.

I slammed the folder closed and slapped it on the coffee table. I probably had the evidence of whatever Eileen had found and I couldn't read it! A bubble rose in my throat. I belched pink stuff and old beer.

Throwing myself back on the couch, I dug at memories. Eileen had come home furious the Bison directors had picked Harper as a Vice President. Why? She hadn't liked his work ethic, whatever the hell that meant. I remembered telling her to complain to her dad, since he was the big honcho. She rolled her eyes and gave me one of those "You don't know what you're talking about" looks. Maggie had said this file was all about Eileen's investigation of the death of Mrs. Harper. The husband VP was waiting to collect a five hundred thousand dollar policy . . . waiting on Eileen to verify the facts of his wife's death. Only Eileen had found something suspicious. She had told Maggie that Harper may have contributed to the death . . . for the insurance. That would be one murder. What would prevent him from going for two? Greed led to the first murder . . . if that's what the files in front of me proved. But how would that connect him to Eileen being shot down in a robbery of a convenience store . . . as in conveniently shot down.

The Giorgio Italian shoes flashed into my mind. I stiffened. Bang! The memory crap had gone far enough. I sat up, opening and closing my shaking hands. My eyes settled on the folders littering the low table before me. I stared at the one holding the computer prints-outs. Damn stuff was like a foreign language! Who did I know who spoke "computer?"

Maggie, of course. But she wasn't home. At least she hadn't answered her phone. I had called her shortly after midnight. She was not exactly a party animal. So why wasn't she home?

I looked at my watch. Six a.m. Where the hell was Lori? Driving Henry around all night? Hardly! She mentioned he expected her to take him to some sort of "spooky" place. Why hadn't I asked her what that meant? Probably because my gut instinct told me not to hint that she could take care of herself.

I walked to the desk and dialed Maggie's number again. She

should be up and getting ready for work. On the fourth ring, a man's voice answered, "Miss Holmes's residence."

A man? With Maggie? I guessed that explained why she didn't answer her phone last night. My mind couldn't create an image of someone taking Maggie Holmes to bed. On the other hand, if there was anything Harry and Lori had taught me, it was the world was full of all kinds of people.

I shook myself to get back to business. "May I speak to Maggie, please? It's important."

"May I ask who's calling?"

"Bob Norris."

"Well, hello, Mr. Norris. You seem to be popping up every time someone dies lately."

"What are you talking about? Who is this?"

"Detective Sergeant Morten. When was the last time you talked to Miss Holmes?"

Panic rose inside me. "Where is she?"

"Right here . . . but she's dead. Sorry I didn't tell you sooner."

My fingers tried to bury themselves in the plastic of the receiver. "Thanks, asshole, for being so sensitive about it. Are you going to tell me how she . . . died . . . or do I have to read it in the papers?"

"You're asking me questions? Wrong. I'll do the asking. Let me repeat . . . When did you last talk to Miss Holmes?"

"About two weeks ago."

"Did she say anything about having problems, maybe a stalker or something?"

"No." I dropped into the desk chair, rubbing my forehead to clear the shock from my stressed brain.

"Did she have enemies? Anyone who might want to kill her?"

"God! She's been murdered! How?"

"Shot. She was found in bed with one hand on the phone. No forcible entry either. How did you know the victim?"

"She was my wife's secretary . . . Ah, Morten, has her apartment been ransacked, torn up, anything out of order?"

"Not a thing. Should there be?"

Think fast, Big Mouth! Why the hell are you asking him of all people? "Because she was very tidy . . . a neat-freak. That's why Eileen depended on her. If there is . . . anything that looks messy . . . I just thought you might want to look there for clues."

"You're being helpful. Why don't I believe that? Let's make this official. You will make a statement . . . about everything you know about the victim and your last meeting, conversation, whatever. Is that clear enough?"

"Morten, this woman . . . was a friend. All right? You just told me she was found shot to death in her apartment. Now, Pig, you want a statement, you come to my place or get a warrant and drag me to yours!" I slammed the phone down before he could reply.

For long minutes I sat with my elbows braced on the desk, my face buried in my hands. Lori wasn't home to talk to. Harry was sleeping off his beer . . . and Lori hadn't been there last night to remind him of his pills. I couldn't handle waking him in the middle of a battle with some Viet Cong. My own mental battles were bad enough.

Why? Obvious, Norris. Eileen . . . then Maggie . . . now you are in to some deep shit!

Looking at the files on the coffee table reminded me of my challenge to Morten. I felt like a coward shoving them back in the box and carrying it to the closet. If this was evidence in a murder, the police needed to see it. Eventually. But not Morten. I had to know what information was in those print-outs first.

How was I going to do that? Who would help me? After enough crap had been piled on top of the container, I let my gaze roam the closet. On the shelf at eye-level, I found a box labeled "East High," That box ended up on the desk.

I didn't know squat about computers. I even gave my grades and other paperwork to the secretary of the Fine Arts Department. She entered my stuff for me. I intended to take a summer semester in something called "Digital Animation," a computer art course. Logically, it would fulfill my mandatory continuing education and move me into the computer age. Two summers in a row I had registered and canceled. To me, art meant sketching, chalks, pastels, oils . . . not goddamn computers.

In the middle of the junk crammed in the box, I found the East High Faculty directory for the past year. Remembering the secretary as a classic gossip, I skipped her. Under Technology/Practical Sciences I found the heading "Computers." Seeing it listed with "Home Economics" and "Industrial Technology" made me cringe. That was about as far from Fine Arts as the human mind could get.

My finger stopped on the name "Donaldson, Edward." Tall, muscular, athletic, what the females in the student body and staff called a "hunk." Unmarried, too, and nothing like a stereo-typical computer geek. We shared the same lunch period last year. He told damn good jokes and enjoyed playing poker against his computer. He also got a kick out of trying to teach me how to do both and my predictable failure. This project might interest him. Anyway, I hoped it would. After four rings, his answering machine kicked in. Why did I expect a teacher to be up early during summer vacation? I left a message.

A crash sounded in Harry's room, followed by a garbled shout and distinct curses. He was up. This waking-dream battle lasted a bit longer than the other episodes, forty-five minutes. I kept checking my watch as I tried once again to read that novel from the safety of the couch.

Finally, the shouts and thumping stopped. Minutes dragged by. I could imagine him rubbing his aching head and looking around at his trashed room. The silence was broken by the flap of Harry's slippers on the wood floor as he headed to the kitchen. Tap water ran. He emerged through the doorway, holding a glass of water in his shaking hand. I studied the torn man calmly sitting down at the dining table. Perspiration sheened his scarred face. His sleeveless t-shirt stuck to his chest and back.

For the first time I saw the stump of his left arm. Always before he wore long-sleeved shirts with that sleeve pinned up. The military doctors had sliced off the arm just below the shoulder joint. Deep scars ran up from the puckered flesh, disappearing under the t-shirt. On second thought, surgeons knives hadn't done all that. I decided they probably tried their best to line up the pieces of a puzzle. It hadn't quite worked.   Harry looked at me over the glass as he took a swallow of water. "What's the matter? Never seen a man in boxer shorts before?"

"You forgot to take your pills again."

"Did I sound bad?"

"Maybe a little worse than normal."

"Why are you up so early? We came in pretty late last night . . . I think."

"Yeah, well. My brain wouldn't shut down." I filled him in on Maggie's message on the answering machine, my discovery of the computer garbage, and Morten's news.

"Where'd you put the print-outs?"

"Box in the closet. I didn't want it out if the asshole comes for me."

"Let me see 'em."

I started to laugh, but he cocked an eyebrow that told me to get my butt in gear. Digging through that closet was getting to be a habit. I left the junk on the floor, opened the box where it was, and pulled out the print-outs, still all neatly fan-folded together. Remaining at the table, Harry took the folder from me.

"Gonna leave that crap there for us to stumble over?"

"No. When you get done, I'll put it all right back where I had it, on top of the box to hide it!"

"You need a housekeeper, Norris!"

"There's you or Lori. Who would you appoint?"

He shrugged and turned to expertly examine the print-outs.

"You can make any sense out of it?"

"Besides your wife's notes? Naw. I need a computer . . . and the disc that matches these pages."

I went back to the box and rummaged around. My fingers slid over thin, hard plastic. I held it up. "What do you think?"

"Bingo!"

"So, how do you know about this computer shit?"

He dropped back in his chair, one finger playing with the edges of the print-outs, his eyes staring at nothing. "Went to City College on the G.I. Bill. A piece of paper says I learned something . . . an associate degree in office management."

"You're kidding!" I regretted the words the minute they slid from my mouth. I had known the man for two years, but never bothered to really know him.

He shrugged again then closed the file in front of him.

"I didn't mean it that way, Harry. I just . . . Well, why are you working in a convenience store?"

"Hiring the handicapped ain't a priority in the business world. Scarred . . . and maimed people make everyone nervous. That's not good for business. So . . . do you know where we can borrow a computer?"

"Maybe I can just buy one . . . if my father-in-law left me enough money."

The phone rang. I grabbed it up.

"Hi, there!" Lori spoke before I could even say anything.

"Where the hell are you?"

"I just dropped Henry at Ashland Steel. I'm beat and I need a shower and some sleep. Did you hear about Charles?"

My heart dropped into my stomach. I couldn't handle one more murder this morning. "No, I haven't talked to the hospital."

A horn blared in the background. "Up yours!" Lori shouted. "Sorry, I'm not used to talking on the phone and driving a tank with one hand. Henry was out and about most of the night, pretty good for a man his age. I kept dozing off."

"You were going to tell me about Chucky."

"Charles, remember? Well, he ran away from the hospital. Skipped out without anybody seeing him. Nobody knows where he's at."

"You're kiddin' me! When?"

"Hospital called Henry about an hour ago. Said he left between three and four. They had to search the entire place before notifying the party responsible for him, or his bill more likely. And that was Henry. But . . . he's not pissed. Ain't that strange? He put on a show that he cared so damn much. He didn't even act surprised."

The old man probably blamed me for Chucky's behavior, since

he blamed me for everything else. It was a wonder he hadn't called with one of his I-told-you-so messages. "If Henry was up all night, he probably put his brain on auto-pilot and could give a shit about anybody else."

"Your father-in-law is weird, Bob. Know where I took him last night?" Horn honking. "Damn! Can't throw him the finger! Where was I . . . Geesh, I'm so tired, I'm getting dopey. Oh, yeah. The Pink Horn. He called it the Gentleman's Club. And he had the balls to ask me to go in with him."

Henry and Lori. Now, that was tough to imagine. "What kind of a place is it, a strip joint?"

"That I wouldn't have minded . . . but . . . ah, did you know Henry's gay?"

The phone dropped from my hand. I fumbled it like a slippery fish.

"What's going on?" Harry insisted.

"Shut up!" I recovered and tried to sound in control. "Well, ah, no, that is not something I knew. Never crossed my mind . . . even." Motion picture visions in my mind rolled right along with my stomach. At that moment I hated my vivid artist's imagination! "Not that I'm prejudiced—"

"Maybe not prejudiced, but you don't like it around you, right?"

"Henry's business is his business, Lori. And you didn't sound so thrilled about the Pink Horn."

"You sitting, Bob? A friend of mine works there, a gay guy. He's big, well-built, works out with weights—"

"I get the picture!"

"He's suited to the Pink Horn, 'cause the clients are in to S and M, the heavy S and M, if you get my meaning."

"I know what S and M is! I am an adult male!"

"That so, Mr. Smart Aleck. Well, the adult males partying in that joint like their pain with their pleasure, bad pain. Think you're man enough for that scene, I'll take you there myself!"

"Ha, ha! Very funny. And no thanks."

"Aw, I'm too beat, anyway . . . Get it? Beat?" When he didn't laugh, she gave him the raspberries over the phone. "No sense of humor, Norris, no matter what Henry says! I'll be home in about ten minutes. Think I could park this thing in the garage?"

"No other tenants that I've seen. Enough room. But, Harry and I won't be here. We're going to buy a computer."

Early that afternoon, Harry completed plugging in the wires and hesitated just a moment to admire the most expensive, most powerful computer Business Express sold. The plastic-encased brain and its companion printer took up the top of my precious desk. Harry had picked up an adapter so we could use the existing phone line to access the Internet.

The man's whole personality changed as he sat down in the desk chair and began familiarizing himself with programs, whatever that meant. He sat with his shoulders back as he confidently tapped keys and manipulated the plastic lump called a mouse. Control! This was something he had the power to control, instead of complying with the demands of others, even my demands.

For a moment I cringed that I had fallen into that world of manipulative people, but quickly squelched the idea. Harry had made the choice to help me. He didn't have to be here, whereas I did. I was driven. I would do whatever it took to find out who had destroyed a vital part of my life and why. I frowned at Harry with the realization he had taken on my cause. Maybe because he didn't have anything better to do.

"Harry?"

"Yeah?" he mumbled.

"Why are you doing this, I mean all this?"

He hesitated, but didn't look at me. "Tired of senseless bullshit that hurts innocent people." He tapped at keys, pushed the mouse, leaned back and stared at the changing screen. "In my nightmares . . . well, I live it over, I think, 'cause I want to change what happened. It never works. Here . . ." his hand indicated the entire room. ". . . maybe I can keep your sorry ass from getting killed. Then again maybe I can't, but at least I can try. Right?"

"You and Lori aren't very reassuring, you know that? She thinks the street will kill me. You think I'm going to piss somebody off as I get too close."

"What do I know? You're college-educated and teacher. I'm just a leach on society . . . well, that's what my ol' lady told me a while back."

Screeches and beeps sounded from the computer. "What's that?"

He grinned up at me. "I just got into a public access bulletin board, and now . . ." He leaned toward the screen. ". . . I'll find Bison Insurance."

"What! I thought you were going to just look at Eileen's disc."

"What good will that do, if there's no data to compare it to?"

I cocked my head at him. "How should I know? I'm just a college-educated jerk. You're the computer geek!"

A grin spread over his lips, as he tapped at keys. "A jerk and a geek, huh? And both crazy as hell. That's Lori's opinion, anyway."

I glanced at my watch. She had wanted me to get her up at two. Henry had a four o'clock appointment.

Harry slid Eileen's disc into the computer. He scrolled the files named by number, focused on one, and clicked the mouse. "Access Denied" appeared on the screen.

"Damn!" He slapped the side of the monitor.

"So you can't get into it?"

"Could take me hours, or even days. She used some access code."

"Oh, yeah. I forgot to tell you." His expression was not pleased. "Maggie told me about it. I found it in my car, but, ah, well I gave it to Maggie then burned it."

"Save me from an education if it makes somebody as dumb as you!"

"Ha, Ha! An education is supposed to teach you how to think, not what to think! My mind just happens to focus on images, instead of orderly things, god dammit! Just give me a minute." I closed my eyes to block out his disgusted expression, as much as to play back that night I gave the code to Maggie. "Got it! B-N-6-1-5!" He started to tap. "Wait! Maggie intended to change it, for safety's sake."

"Great! Then she got herself dead!" The fingers of his only hand punched keys a little harder.

Deflated, I noticed it was time to get Lori up. I called through her door. No answer. Still nothing to my knock, so I opened the door. She lay in a sprawl on the bed, naked and softly snoring, a fly circling inches from her childlike, sleeping face. Feeling like a voyeur, I looked over her exposed curves and creamy skin. How could any woman want to sell something so beautiful? To eat, to survive, College Man! I remembered the three thousand she had taken off Alabama. When is it enough? Maybe when some- one learns they can do something else . . . like Harry and the computer? So what could Lori learn to do? And why is it any of your business, Norris? Because you changed her options, Idiot! Now what?

My groin began to ache. I rubbed my hand across my eyes and yelled "Lori! God dammit! It's time to get up!"

Startled and immediately on the defensive, she rolled, grab- bing sheets and bedspread to cover herself. I left the room.

Harry's concentration had him hunched forward.

"Any luck?"

"No. How about you?"

"What'd you mean?"

"Were you just looking or touching?"

"Looking. Period! That's all I will do and you know it!"

"Frustrating as hell, ain't it? 'Cause that's all I'm getting done here. I need to know Maggie's change."

"No way to break into the file? I mean, I've heard about com- puter hackers—"

"I didn't say I was a friggin' genius, Bob!"

"Coffee made?" Lori asked.

We both turned to find her in t-shirt and tight jeans, her fingers buried in her sleep-tousled hair.

"No, ah—" I stuttered.

"Why don't you make us all some?" Harry casually turned back to his computer screen.

I watched her walk toward the kitchen. She turned on the TV in passing. A moment later I heard one of those "News we're working on . . ." announcements followed by "Margaret Holmes, a single woman living alone, is an another murder victim in the growing list of criminal deaths plaguing this city. Apparently the burglar shot her three times while she lay sleeping in her bed. Also add to the list, an unidentified male pulled from the Missouri River. The man appears to be in his late sixties and was wearing a chauffeur's uniform. More details at five."

Harry's gaze slowly swung up to mine. I dropped into one of the dining room chairs. Lori stood in the kitchen doorway, her eyes shiny and round.

"It's Charles, isn't it?" She whispered.

Something tightened in my chest then hardened. I stared at Harry. "We are going to find out what is happening here, by God! If this Frank Harper is behind whatever it is, I want his ass."

Harry nodded solemnly as he punched computer keys and shut the thing down. He had no sooner stood up than the phone rang. He picked it up and handed it to me on his way to the kitchen.

"Robert? Is that you?"

"Yes, Henry. What do you want?"

"I've been trying to get through to you, but your line's been busy. Something terrible . . . The police want me to identify . . . They think Charles committed suicide, jumped in the Missouri River."

"I just heard on TV they found a body in a chauffeur's uniform. Said he was unidentified—"

"Weren't you listening? That's what they want me to do! It's . . . incredible! Why would the man kill himself?"

That finally registered. "Yeah, why would he do that? Hard to believe. Will you be handling arrangements?"

"Of course, not! I called his family in Wisconsin. Well, I may have a memorial . . . or something. I've tried to reach Lori on the car phone. Do you know—"

"She stopped by here and fell asleep."

"If she is truly his niece, she will want to know of course."

"Of course."

"But, please tell her I do need her to take up Charles' responsibilities until I can hire a suitable replacement."

I rubbed my eyes. "Back up, Henry. You knew Lori was here. You know who she is."

"I didn't attain my position and power by accident, Robert. I do not tolerate being played the fool. I knew from the beginning. I just wanted to see how long you all wanted to play the identity game and why."

"Would it surprise you to know we did it for Chucky, ah, Charles?"

"Knowing what a sentimental fool you are? Not really."

"If we're into confessions here . . . Before I put her on the phone, what's with you and the Pink Horn?"

"Ah, so she's also spying on my private life . . . which happens to be none of your business. The Pink Horn is a sanctuary of sorts, a place I escape the pressures of all that position and power of mine. Get a drink, smoke a cigar, take a restful nap."

"Bullshit, Henry! You forget who Lori is and her connections. It's a goddamn queer joint and they do nasty things there."

"And your point, Robert?" I heard a heavy sigh and knew he was rubbing the bridge of his nose like he always did when trying to be patient with lesser people. "Their establishment has two separate areas, one provides tasteful entertainment, the other is reputedly, oh, wilder, shall we say. But, the bottom line is that my patronage is still my business, my private business. Charles respected that and I expect Lori to do the same or her employment will be very short. Since you have become her dear friend, do you want to explain those financial facts of life, or should I?"

"It's your money, Henry. I'll let you do the honors."

Chapter Eleven

A seductive smile is a tough thing to ignore, but I was on to Lori. She used her "wares" when she either wanted me to do something or she knew something she didn't want me to know. She sat across the dining room table with that smile. I sipped my coffee and tried to remember how I used to deal with teenage girls in the classroom who pulled the same stuff. This was more irritating because Lori knew what I had going.

As if I had not heard her the first time, she repeated herself. "He lied to you. Henry did not know me until he came out of the Pink Horn. Someone in there recognized me and told him."

I resisted the urge to call the bastard. He would only get pissed off and take another thousand out off my allowance. Why would he lie about knowing Lori? To divert my attention from his sexual preferences? Hadn't he made it clear my opinion didn't matter, one way or the other?

Harry spooned more sugar into his coffee. "So, are you going to drive for him or not?"

She shrugged. "Why not? I can pick up some gossip and get paid. What have I got to lose?"

"Your ass, Lori," I reminded her. "You do what you want. Just know that old man knows only one word, 'Yes.'"

"I think maybe that's why Charles ended up in the river."

We drank our coffee in silence. Since the three of us were together, I decided we needed to discuss our next move.

"Harry, do you think this Frank Harper had something to do with killing Eileen?"

"Yeah, he would be my first suspect, Bob."

"To cover up the insurance fraud?"

"Yup, I'd say so . . . but he wasn't in the Stop and Go that day. Big shots usually hire scumbags to do it for them. I bet he also sent someone to that secretary's apartment. I can tap into some Bison computer logs, find out if anybody was checking up on her . . . and if she changed Eileen's access code. It may lead back to Harper . . ."

He shrugged.

"So you're into all that computer shit, huh? I never woulda guessed." Lori blinked those big eyes at him.

Harry sat up a little straighter. "I got all kinds of talent you don't know about."

"I ain't no talent agent, fella!"

Before they totally changed back to their street talk, I jumped in. "Lori, does Henry go to Bison, like on a regular basis?"

"I'm just his driver, not his friggin' secretary."

"Okay! But have you taken him there?"

"Yeah, once. He had a board meeting. Ordered me to get coffee in the employee cafeteria. I didn't even have to pay."

"So you were allowed into the building?"

She smirked at me then went into that smile again. "I get it! You want me to find this guy Harper . . . well, his office. If I'm caught, should I say I was hired to 'entertain' Mr. Harper?"

Harry choked on his coffee.

I just rolled my eyes. "Depends on who catches you, I guess, and what you're doing at the time."

Lori leaned on her elbows and thought about that. "This could be . . . fun. Say, I wonder if Henry has an office there, too."

"No, he's just on the board. Why do you ask?"

"I saw a fancy assed office in a movie one time. That one had a bedroom, bathroom, bar, the works just like a high priced hotel. Thought Henry might keep clothes there like he does at the Pink Horn."

"He keeps clothes at the gay place? Who told you that?"

"My friend there. It's not like Henry as a room of his own. He just has this suitcase of clothes. And Bernie said they joke about his passport and a million bucks being locked up in the safe—"

"For a quick get away," Harry interrupted. I frowned at him. "Think about it, Bob! Why would he keep clothes in a place like that, unless he wants to go in and disappear out the back."

"Better question is 'Why would he want to?'"

"Bobby Boy, I think we are getting into deeper shit than Eileen being shot in my convenience store."

"Yeah." I sipped my coffee, feeling over-whelmed and not liking it. Too late now, Norris! "So, either of you want out?"

"Hell no!" They chorused, then laughed.

"So, Lori, when you drive Henry to Bison next time—"

"If I last that long. He told me flat out that he didn't think I would be suitable for 'long term employment.' He's advertising for a 'professional like Charles.'"

"In other words, someone I am not connected with, the bastard!"

The front door vibrated under a loud knock. Nobody moved.

"Would you answer it, Harry?"

"No."

"Why not?"

"I'm a computer operator now, not a goddamn butler. Anyway, whoever it is, they'd ask for you. I haven't gotten a call or a visitor since I been here. Neither has Lori! Your door. You answer it!"

I stomped across the living room and yanked it open without checking the peep hole, like the two people at the table had drilled into me. Worm stared at me. I took a step back from his body odor.

"Fox sent me."

"I would ask you in, but I'm out of room deodorant." The hall would hold his smell, though. For a second I thought of the run to the elevator holding my breath. The image died when I saw his eyes narrow. "So, what does Fox want?"

"You . . . to meet him at the Tickled Pink in one hour."

I checked my watch then glanced over at Harry. He nodded his head once. "Okay, sure. Tell him I'll be there."

Worm pointed a cocked finger at me before turning. I closed the door, my hand fanning the air under my nose. Harry headed to the bathroom while Lori picked up our cups.

"What do you make of that?" I asked her.

"Harry and me agreed Fox would've killed you a long time ago, if he wanted. A word of advice: Be on time. I'll carry these in the kitchen . . . but like Harry said about the door, it's your place, you wash 'em. I've got to get ready to pick up Henry. Don't wait up.

Remember he's a party animal. Animal. Get it?"

"Spare me your sick wise-cracks . . . and be careful. Something weird is going on. Until we figure it out . . . I don't know. Don't put yourself in a corner."

"Ah, you care," she said with exaggerated sarcasm. "I'm the one rubbing elbows with the rich. You're the one meeting the city's dirtiest pimp." She switched her rear at me on her way to the kitchen.

I sat on the couch just staring at that damn paperback, thinking how Lori had contrasted the rich and the pimp, I wondered which kind was more dangerous, especially in the game we seemed to be playing. My stomach rolled. A game where people ended up dead was not exactly . . . a game.

The scent of spicy aftershave got my attention. Harry stood beside me, working the buttons of a clean shirt, the one long sleeve neatly pinned up.

"On your way to work?"

"Have to go in early. The afternoon clerk isn't coming in. Some damn poor excuse."

"When did you find that out?"

"Supervisor called while you were in the can."

"So you do know how to answer the phone?"

He went out the door without bothering to answer.

Lori emerged from her bedroom wearing the tailored uniform.

"Want a lift? The limo might impress Fox."

We trotted down the hall to the elevator. When the doors opened on a higher concentration of Worm's smell, without a word we both turned to the stairs.

In the almost deserted garage, I slid into the passenger side of the front seat. The soft leather felt good and smelled better. Lori gunned it as we left the garage ramp, hydroplaning across the sidewalk and dropping onto the street with a rocking bounce. Mostly because of the rain, I buckled myself into the seatbelt. When she took the corner too wide, I stared into the rain-glare of oncoming headlights, gulped, and grabbed the dashboard. She swerved. My foot stomped invisible brakes. The swing around another corner headed the limo down a less traveled street.

"What's your goddamn hurry? You want to kill us?"

"I don't bitch 'bout the way you drive!"

"And I bet you don't drive like this when Henry's in the car!"

She squinted through the wiper blades and hit the brakes. A horn sounded behind us. Her finger pointed. "Tickled Pink."

"Call me on the car phone later, if you want to find out what Fox says."

"Yeah, and you can find out if poor lil' ol' me has survived the city streets."

"You get funnier every time you open your mouth, Lori."

"And you don't! I can drive and I can take care of myself, hayseed!"

The limo tires squealed as I slammed the door shut.

Inside, I headed toward the empty table under the cowboy painting. Pam waved as I passed. She bent over the nearby table, her skimpy shorts showing more than they covered. At the table, I pulled out a chair and faced the entrance, like Harry had taught me. I pictured myself in a western hat, brim pulled down, my hand on the gun at my hip, my spurs and boots propped on the table. Too much, Norris. Gotta be ready to move. Not a game. Not a game. Not a . . . .

A short, fat man walked in. He slid onto a barstool like a regular customer. Pam called out to a couple coming through the door. I looked at my watch. Fox was late.

"You're still drinking from the tap, right?" Pam asked as she set a glass of the cheap beer in front of me. She smiled as if she knew moving my gaze from her skimpy halter top to her face strained my optic nerves. "Where's everyone else?"

"Ah, working. I'm here, ah, waiting for someone."

"Need a pitcher then?"

"No." I resisted the urge to burp at the thought of it. "Oh, I see Worm coming in now."

"You ain't going to drink with that sonofabitch are you?"

"Not if I can help it. I'm waiting on Fox."

She rolled her eyes. "Thanks for the warning. I'll be right back with his drink."

Worm stepped back out the door. A moment later, a broad-shouldered man with a full head of thick curls entered and walked directly toward me. The dim bar lighting shadowed the long scar reaching from just below his left eye, across his nose and down the right cheek to his chin. Considering his size, I tried to imagine what he did to his attacker in return for that scar. Then I remembered the one time I had seen him at parent-teacher conferences. What I had imagined then was tame to what I imagined now.

Fox sat across from me, angled so he too could look up at the door.

"Want a beer?"

"No thanks." His raspy voice didn't sound so intimidating outside the close quarters of his Lincoln and, of course, he wasn't holding a shotgun. "Can't drink the stuff. Eats my stomach. The broad at the bar is getting my usual."

Silence fell as Pam placed a tall glass of milk in front of him.

I waited until she moved off. "For your ulcers?"

"Ain't got ulcers. I just like my scotch mixed with this stuff, Norris," he leaned forward, his voice dropping, "I found a guy who can talk to you about your wife."

I sat up straighter, my chest tight. "Okay. Appreciate it. Can you take me to him?"

"No, you have to go on your own. Don't want him knowing that I sicced you on him . . . unless you need to pressure him."

"You could have called me and told me that. My phone works fine."

"Relax, Norris. You look uncomfortable here. I just wanted to get to know you a little better."

I took a long drink of the beer. "Excuse me, but you wanted to kill me. Remember?"

"History. Misunderstanding. Thought we got that straight. Found out I owed you and now I'm making good my debt."

Finishing the beer, I leaned my elbows on the table and lowered my own voice. "So tell me about this guy."

"His name is Trout. He picks up petty cash at gas stations and corner stores, if you get me. I think you met him . . . when he pointed his shotgun at your one-armed friend."

"You think he'll tell me who the other gunman was?"

Fox shrugged. "Depends on how tough you come off."

"How do I find this Trout?"

"He's got a routine. Gets off work at eleven and stops at the Alibi Bar."

"He works?" My voice rose a notch. "You mean he has a god-damn job? I thought he held up places."

Fox's big hand squeezed my arm to quiet me. "That's his job, Norris. He's a stick-up man who puts in regular hours. Sometimes he's just watching and planning a hit. Then he does his thing. But he puts in regular hours. His wife thinks he's got an honest profession, doing some kind of messenger service."

In silence, Pam sat down another milk-'n-Scotch and beer then took our empty glasses. We waited until she reached the bar.

"So where's the Alibi?" I asked.

"Down by the river, on the corner of Third and Poppleton. I'm feeling like a burger and fries. How about you?"

Over the next couple of hours, I learned about Fox's territory, his interests beyond pimping, and his sincere pride in his son. I also learned he ignored the hamburger fat dripping from his chin and his disgusting treatment of cigars. He liked to deep-throat the brown cylinder, then twist it around in his mouth. Pulling it out, he bit off the end and carelessly spit that on the floor. He then moved the flame of a silver-plated lighter back and forth along the length of the cigar. Once he finally lit the smelly weed, he puffed like a steam engine until a cloud surrounded his head and me.

Between the raunchy beer, the greasy burgers, and his cigar, I imagined myself pouring gasoline over him. Then he stirred my sympathy with talk of his family, how he visited his totally straight wife at least once a week and how he phoned his son every Sunday evening, without fail. In the next breath he launched into the details of his business rounds. He checked his girls every half hour. If they weren't at their assigned spot, he assumed they were making money.

On the next round, he collected their earnings. As if instructing me in how to handle whores, he emphasized the easy record keeping of who was up and who was down. The third time he repeated his stories I realized he was drunk, but didn't care because I had become his friend. I wondered what Henry would think of me being a close friend to the city's leading pimp. I burped the cheap beer then laughed. Fox pounded me on the back and laughed, too.

When Worm appeared at the table, I appreciated the smoke for the first time all evening. Fox threw some money on the table, shook my hand, and left with his street man to begin his rounds.

My watch showed 11:05. I waved down an empty cab and a few minutes later walked into the Alibi. Billiard balls clacked, chairs creaked, and low voices mumbled. Against the back wall, a lamp hung over a long fooz ball table. The two men playing there looked serious. The place even had two dart boards. The group playing there weren't laughing either. Still, the variety of entertainment beat the loud music and two video games at the Tickled Pink. I thought Lori and Harry might like this for a change of pace.

Sliding onto a barstool, I tried to be casual as I looked over the men in the place. My neck muscles tightened. Could I pick out the man who held the shotgun? Or would I have to ask? And would that make someone suspicious? Time isn't giving you choices, Norris!

"What'll you have?" The round-faced bartender wore a faded yellow apron over a dirty t-shirt.

"Whatever you've got on tap." As he filled a glass, I jumped in. "Is there a guy here named Trout?"

The bartender's eyes narrowed. "What ya want to know for?"

"I need a job. Heard he sometimes hires a helper."

His gaze swept over my clothes. "He's at the end of the bar, wearing the Chicago Cub ball cap."

I took my beer down the bar and slid onto the stool beside Trout. The bartender watched as he washed glasses at the other end of the bar. I caught the hint of a nod he gave Trout. The man blew smoke in my face and stared at me. In the low lighting I couldn't tell if his eyes looked cold, but they felt cold.

"Mind if I sit here?"

"I don't give a damn where you sit." I recognized the voice. "It's a free country, dip-shit."

"Bartender said you're Trout."

"Why do you want to know?"

"I lost a wallet a few weeks ago. I heard on the streets you may have it."

"Really?" He blew more smoke. "So who the hell are you?"

"Some people call me Picasso . . ." He put out his cigarette. ". . . but you can call me Mr. Norris."

"What makes you think I got your wallet?"

"Oh, you were short of cash at a Stop-and-Go. You sort of borrowed from me."

His big hand shot out, catching and twisting the front of my T-shirt. I heard a rip as he lifted then slammed me against the bar. My ears rang. The next instant a hand pressed my face into the counter surface, crunching my nose. Something hard pressed into my temple. I didn't think it was a finger.

A nasty whisper sounded next to my ear, "Tell me why you're here or I'll blow your goddamn brains out your left ear!"

Wishing I had used the restroom before talking to him, I tried to call up all those lessons from Harry and Lori. What the hell would Picasso say? "The bartender would get real pissed. Think of the mess he'd have to clean up."

Laughter sounded around me. Witnesses! No, asshole they're laughing at you!

"His balls are bigger than his brain, Trout."

The pressure at my temple disappeared. The hand released me. I carefully sat up. Trout still held his gun on me, but the bartender and on-lookers drifted away, obviously aware this was a private matter.

"Who sent you?"

"Fox."

His bottom lip twitched. Without looking away from my face, he slid his gun back in its shoulder holster under his denim vest. He shrugged then relaxed against the bar, twirling his beer bottle between his hands. "Why would Fox do that?"

"He said you could help me."

Trout sucked on the green-tinted glass. *He drinks expensive foreign made shit, while I drink piss beer?*

"And how does the Big Man want me to help you?"

"Do you remember the Stop-and-Go?"

"Yeah, like it was yesterday."

"Tell me the name of the man who killed my wife. I'll walk out of here and you'll never see or hear from me again."

"When was that? The Stop-and-Go I remember was yesterday."

My back stiffened. *I was not going to be manipulated by some petty ante bastard. That was one lesson Fox had taught me!*

My voice came out low and hard. "You and another man walked into a Stop-and-Go at 120th and Dodge. You pushed me to the floor and took my wallet . . . while the other man shot my wife. Now do you remember, you sonofabitch?"

He didn't move, but his eyes flicked side to side to see if anyone was nearby.

"I don't care about the money," I continued. "I want the man who murdered Eileen."

"You're that school teacher. You ain't Picasso."

"Right and wrong. I'm the school teacher who became Picasso. Don't screw with me. You have no idea the influence I have over the streets, even over Fox."

He swallowed hard, wet his lips, barely nodded, and began to talk. "I-I don't know the guy well. Only seen him once since the holdup. Before that I was with him every day for two weeks, even then he was a closed-mouth bastard. We followed the woman, ah, your wife, I guess . . . we followed her for two weeks. Drove my old Chevy van down town. Never went into her fancy neighborhood. Too easy to spot, he said."

I motioned for him to hurry up.

"That day the guy was real nervous. We watched her get in your fancy car outside the insurance place. When you walked into that

Stop-and-Go, he decided at the last minute to pull a hold-up. Sudden-like, he iced your wife. I-I had no idea he was going to do that. Honest, Mister..ah, Picasso."

My jaw clamped. "His name and where I can find him."

"Wait a minute, here. I'm a professional. He paid me a grand to just drive around and I got to keep the holdup money. My time's worth—"

"How much?"

His confidence returned. "Six big ones."

"Let's get this business transaction clear. Are you saying you want six thousand dollars to give me a name and tell me where I can find him?"

"Yeah, that's right. That's what I have to have, in cash. I got a reputation to protect. You should know that."

"I'll have it tomorrow night."

Chapter Twelve

Eileen lifted a pointing finger, not at me but at something beyond my shoulder. I was just turning to see when the slam of Harry's door jerked me awake.

My tongue stuck to the roof of my mouth. I burped.

"God! I gotta start drinking with Trout. The cheap stuff is killing me!" I mumbled on my way to the bathroom.

In the kitchen, I gratefully found Harry's medicine bottles open beside the sink. His plastic glass had been dropped on top of the growing pile of dirty dishes. Damn! I wondered how much a dishwasher cost and when I could get one installed.

After downing a couple gulps of the pink stuff, I dialed Henry's office and waited, hand pressed against my forehead.

"Yes, Robert. What now?" His irritating voice demanded.

"I need six thousand dollars."

"That's ridiculous!" Computer keys clicked. "My records indicate you used up your allowance for the month. Looks like a computer store purchase took the last of it. I'm not advancing any more. I warned you. You'll have to wait until next month for any more splurges on your friends."

"Goddamn it, this is important!"

"Not to me. Try someone else!" And he hung up.

A deep breath helped the ache in my head. I refused to let the bastard stop me. My watch read a quarter past eight, so I knew dependable Donald would be at work. One secretary later, I heard his concerned voice.

"Bob! How are you? What's going on?"

"Everything is working out here. I want to know why you froze my bank account on Henry's say so."

"He described your irrational actions and how you were spending your money like a lunatic. I couldn't help but agree. Your financial situation has to be guarded until you recover from Eileen's death."

"What do you mean you agreed? I'm not acting like one of my adolescent students here. I told you I was going to find the killer and I am. Now, you call that perverted bastard and the two of you do whatever needs doing to open my account again!"

"Can't do that, buddy. You don't need this mission, or whatever you want to call it. You need to rest. In a few months, everything will begin to look normal to you—"

"Donald!" I interrupted, then tried to sound calmer. "I am normal now . . . and as sane as I was a year ago. I said things are working out and they are, but I need more money and I need it today."

"How much?"

"Six Thousand."

"Six what?" He hesitated. "Why?"

"To pay a man for information, accurate information on Eileen's murder."

Silence then a sigh. "I'm sorry, Bob. Do you honestly think that sounds rational? I can't help you. If this guy is for real, why don't you turn him over to the police for questioning? Doesn't that sound more reasonable than six thousand dollars?"

I rubbed my head hard, my eyes pinched tight. As much as I had refused to let Henry get to me, hearing Donald's distrust truly hurt. "You're a real brother and I won't forget this."

"Bob—"

I hung up on him. When my eyes opened, I found Lori in her football jersey, a coffee cup held out to me.

"You look like you need it."

"How long have you been home?"

"Most of the night. Henry fired me. I waited at the Tickled Pink from midnight on, hoping you would come in."

"I had been there earlier. I went over to the Alibi on a tip. Talked to a man named Trout. Do you known him?"

"Yeah. He had a news stand at 15th and Harney for years . . . until he got tired of being robbed. The kids doing it got meaner. Haven't seen him much in the past year, but heard he was keeping busy. He has a wife—"

"I heard about her. She thinks he's straight."

"So why did you want to talk to Trout?"

"He held the shotgun on Harry the day Eileen was killed."

"She dropped into a dining room chair and stared at me. "Now he's turned mean. Kinda payback, I guess. Did you tell Harry?"

"No. He'd gone to bed when I got up."

"So how did you find Trout?"

"Fox. At first he didn't want anyone to think he . . . snitched, I guess you might call it. But, we ate and drank and talked, so he didn't mind if I threw his name out."

"Are you kidding me?" Her face brightened with admiration. "You are coming right along, Bob. So, the six thousand . . ." Her hand flicked toward the phone, ". . . you told your brother about, is that for Trout?"

"Yes. He turned me down because I sound crazy and Henry turned me down because he wants to control me. I didn't tell the bastard it was to catch his daughter's killer. He probably wouldn't have cared—"

"I have some money," Lori interrupted. "Not that much, but a chunk of it."

"You can't spend your money on my affairs. Hell, you just lost your job! And I lost you your profession!"

That mischievous, manipulative grin appeared. "Henry fired me, but he is giving me some sort of severance pay . . . until I find some 'legitimate employment.' I can pay some of the rent . . . Wait a minute!" She jumped up and took a piece of paper from the coffee table. "Found this notice on the doorknob. I know this is your place, but with everything going on, I read it. It says the building is under new owners."

I scanned the letter. "This doesn't even say who the new landlord is, just the real estate company and a phone number."

"Trust me, Bob. That only means the rent will go up. I can always go back to hooking. Maybe with your connections with Fox now—"

"Shut up, Lori!"

She shrugged just as the bathroom door opened on the sound of the toilet flushing. Lori set a cup of coffee in front of Harry as he took a chair at the table.

"Couldn't sleep?" she asked, looking closely at his face for any signs of those flashbacks.

"Not with you two jabbering away."

"Your medicine's almost gone. Maybe you need something stronger?"

"Don't know. I'll run out to the VA today and ask. Don't know what needs more help, the tired brain or the battered body. All I do know is I gotta be back at work in about six hours."

"Why's that?" I asked.

"It's Friday. The store I'm in now is the main one in this district. The others bring in their deposits between five and six. The supervisor wants me to count everything and sign off their deposit slips."

"You're bullshitting, right? This outfit doesn't have the stores making daily deposits to a bank?"

"The district store makes the deposit. I put the money in a box until all the stores are accounted for. That's supposed to be about seven. Then I count it all one final time and put it in the floor safe for the district manager pick up on his rounds the next day. Then he deposits the whole kit and caboodle."

My brain lit up like a Christmas tree.

"Santa Claus!" I shouted then ran to my bedroom to dig out my wallet. When I returned waving a scrap of folded napkin, Harry and Lori looked at me like I had developed Rudolph's antlers. I winked, pressed one finger to the side of my nose, and dialed the number written on the napkin.

After two rings a tired, stressed voice answered. "What is it?"

"Roy?"

"Who's this?"

"Bob Norris."

A long moment later, he cleared his throat. "The school teacher or should I say Picasso? What can I do for you?"

"Would you like to call in for the arrest of the guy who's been hitting convenience stores?"

"Sure. What have you got?"

126

"I have yet to set it up, but could you meet me at the Tickled Pink around six?"

"Know what? You are one interesting sonofabitch. I'll be there. But, I'll be real disappointed if you say you're putting the sting on Fox."

"Hardly. You'll be happy. Guaranteed."

"I'll be there!"

I looked up into two sets of wary eyes.

"Did you just call the cops, Bob?" Lori demanded.

I shrugged. "Harry, if someone came into your store tonight and demanded that money box, would you give him any crap?"

He groaned. "Bob, you ain't gonna rob me, are you?"

"No, but I have a plan to get the information I want and get the guy off the streets at the same time . . . without spending a dime of six thousand dollars I don't have."

Harry frowned at Lori. "What the hell is he talking about, girl?"

"He found a snitch who wants the six and Henry won't cough it up. It's the same guy who shoved the shotgun in your face."

Harry's expression changed. The hardness there made Lori shiver. "Who?"

"Trout."

Harry nodded once then turned his icy eyes on me. "So this isn't going to cost you a thing, but what's it going to cost me? Especially, since I'm guessing you want the bastard alive?"

"Nothing but patience," I tried to reassure him. "Trust me. He'll get his and not know what happened in the process."

I picked up the phone again. On the eighth ring, someone at the Alibi answered. It turned out to be just a man working for a cleaning crew. He didn't know anyone named Trout. I drummed my fingers on the desk and thought about calling Fox. Lori drummed her painted nails louder. I looked up at that seductive, know-it-all smile of hers.

"All right. You probably know how to get ahold of Trout, don't you."

She pulled her purse from across the table, the jersey riding up her thighs nicely. After a moment of searching, she pulled out a red address book. Expertly flipping through the pages, she motioned me closer with her head. One painted nail indicated the name "Trout" and his number.

"Why would you have that?" I asked.

"When he had his news stand, I stood on the same street corner. He gave it to me in case he got shot or something, and I could call his wife."

"Small world, huh?" Harry quipped with his most sarcastic grin.

A woman's voice answered.

"Is Trout there?"

She did not answer, but I heard footsteps, then Trout's voice. "Who's this?"

"Don't hang up. A friend of yours gave me your number. I have a . . . situation you would definitely be interested in."

"Who the hell are you?"

"We met last night at the Alibi. Norris? The guy who almost crapped his pants when you pulled the gun."

"Oh, ah, wait a minute." He turned from the phone and told his wife to make some coffee since he might get sent out on special duty for his company. Then he came back on. "So, how's your nose?"

"Bleeding stopped."

"Did, ah, Fox hear about that?"

"No."

"Thanks. Who gave you my number?"

"Can't say. Let's cut the crap and get down to business. You do remember our business, don't you?"

"Six businesses to be exact."

"I've got something better than that." He started to interrupt, but I hurried on. "This place will have more than six thousand dollars, plus it will be an easy hit. Guaranteed."

"I've heard that kinda crap all my life. Guaranteed easy. Nothing is easy."

"Believe what you want but you'll be the loser!"

Silence. "Meet me behind the Alibi in an hour."

"Behind the Alibi. One hour." I replaced the receiver, grinning from ear to ear.

"Harry, I think maybe we created a monster." Lori shook her head.

"You listen to me you happy, sonofabitch, I do this and my supervisor will not know one thing. The cops will not hold the money in evidence. Nothing. You understand? I'm bustin' my balls with Stop-and-Go 'cause I see a future. I don't see no future working with someone who gets more full of himself every minute. Do . . . you . . . understand?"

With a thumbs up, I hurried into the bathroom. For the Alibi's daytime neighborhood, I chose my "Kiss" t-shirt and jeans rather than a Kiwi pullover and Docker slacks. The Ferrari, I figured, was on its own parked around the corner from the bar.

The trash-filled alley looked like something out of a doomsday movie. I tried not to cringe as my athletic shoes squished across the trash left soggy by the rain of the day before. I tried not to breathe in too deeply as the late morning sun warmed things up. I looked around for an inset corner to protect my back, yet a short wall I could slide along to escape, if needed. Harry's little lessons were becoming a habit. I found my spot and waited.

The back door to the Alibi creaked as it opened. Trout stepped out. He lit a cigarette and turned almost full circle before seeing me. The cigarette waved at our surroundings.

"Not what you're used to, I'll bet."

I just stared. He glanced around once more as if assuring himself no one else walked in the alley. I wondered if he was going to kick one of the dumpsters. They looked like something Worm would live in. My stance widened a bit as Trout walked closer, but he stayed in the middle of the alley, as ready to move as I was.

"So you know a place that has lots of money."

"A Stop-and-Go where all the other district stores will bring their deposits."

"That so. Tonight?"

I nodded.

"Which one?"

"Who killed my wife?"

"Tell me the store and the time and I'll tell you his name."

I chuckled then sobered abruptly. "You aren't thinking right, Trout. No wonder you're still a small time crook."

"Okay, Picasso," His lip curled with his sarcasm. "How do you know about all this money?"

My laugh sounded like one of Henry's when he was disgusted with his lesser minions. I didn't know if I liked that, but it got Trout's attention. "Thought you knew all about me. I do have connections and business dealings in this town . . . with people a little more respectable than Fox." I sobered. "I had breakfast with the district supervisor. He had to brag about reorganizing their deposit system."

Trout puffed on his cigarette.

I drew myself up to leave. "I'm obviously wasting my time."

"Wait a minute."

"You have something to tell me?"

"His name's Bill Turner."

"Who the hell is that? Where do I find him?"

"He works as a security guard at Bison Insurance."

Bison again. "How do I know you're telling the truth?"

Trout flicked his cigarette butt into a puddle. "You gotta take my word, just like I gotta take yours."

I lifted my hands in mock surrender. "The downtown Stop-and-Go. All deposits are to arrive by 6:45 p.m."

"It'll just be sitting around in neat piles, waiting for me. Do I look like a fool?"

I resisted the temptation to answer that. "It will be counted one last time between 6:45 and 7:00 then it goes into a floor safe."

"And the guy who locks it up can't get it open again. Right?"

I nodded "So, I guess you better get there before 7:00 . . . Right?"

Lori sprawled on the sofa, watching TV and painting her toe nails with cotton stuffed between her toes. She wore an expensive pair of linen slacks and a filmy blouse, similar to the things Eileen used to buy at Marci's.

"Where's Harry?"

"The doctors."

"Do you know when he'll be home?"

"He didn't say. Just something about the VA docs. 'They tell you to wait all day then give you two minutes of their time.' What happened with Trout?"

"He took the bait. I just hope he doesn't shoot Harry."

"Or vice versa. Did you find out who killed—"

"I got a name," I interrupted her. "I'm going to eat a little lunch then pay a visit to Bison Insurance and a man named Bill Turner."

She didn't react to the name, but puckered her lips and blew on the red nails of one foot. "Don't run off. Roy called a few minutes ago. Said he's on his way over."

I watched her carefully wield the thin brush with its blood red color. My gaze moved to her lips and back to the nail coloring. Do people manufacture that matching color or do women have to waste time doing it themselves? I tried to think of what pigments I would mix to get just that shade. Her hand movement stopped. She stared at me staring at her.

"Ah, nice color. I, ah, was supposed to meet him at six. Did he say what he wanted?"

She clicked off the TV before carefully tugging the cotton separators from between her toes. Swinging her legs to the floor she stood up like a cat stretching every muscle of its body. Her arms and hands extending above her head pushed her breasts against the thin blouse material. She wasn't wearing a bra.

"All dressed up and no place to go." There was that seductive smile again. "Why don't I borrow your car and make that trip to Bison Insurance. I could, oh, fill out a job application and ask for Bill Turner." She stepped up close, her arms sliding up around my neck. "I think I might be less obvious than you, Bobby Boy."

I blew out a tense breath. Why did God give some women the gift to manipulate men . . . and the men let them do it? Well, this man won't let this woman do it.

"I guess that sounds like a better idea than my barging in and choking the life out of the sonofabitch."

She cocked her head side to side. "You wouldn't get within ten feet of him, before he took off."

I pulled her arms from my neck and retreated to the kitchen. Building a bologna sandwich and pouring orange juice occupied my hands.

"Bob," Lori called from the living room, "why do you find me so unattractive?"

I stood at the counter staring at the sandwich. It needed mustard. After applying that, I forced myself to take a big bite. How could I tell a young thing like Lori that I saw her as a velvet petaled violet in an onion patch, an aging onion patch. In reality, she had no business squirming around a den of filthy-minded vipers.

"You can't answer me can you?" she called out.

Deciding to hold my ground in the kitchen, I swallowed the last of the sandwich. "There's several things going on here, Lori. I'm like . . . twenty years older than you. And I'm still in love with my wife. For God's sake, I dream about her every single night. All that will pass with time . . . and getting this whole thing . . . over. You are so beautiful that, well . . . someday I want to paint you so that no one will ever know you were ever a whore—"

"So that's it!" she appeared at the door, her eyes wide with anger. "You don't want anything to really do with me, because I'm a goddamn whore."

"That's not it. And you aren't a whore any more. Remember? That's in the past. Forgotten. My point is Eileen is still with me." I stared at the surface of the juice like it was the surface of the lake in my dream. "The dreams. I'm in this boat with her, fishing or rowing or sometimes digging at the water as if it were dirt. Eileen sits in the other end of the boat watching me, expecting me to do something. I never figure out what she wants—"

"Goddamn you, Norris!" She turned to press her forehead against the kitchen doorway, her little sobs sounding like a cat mewing. "I can't count the number of men I took to bed. Here I have to fall in love with a crazy one who doesn't even want to kiss me! I guess that makes me . . . crazy, too."

My heart rolled in my chest and fell into my stomach. I almost dropped the glass. "You *love* me? Ah, please Lori, please don't do this. I can't feel, can't think, can't be really sane, I guess, while Eileen's still with me."

She looked at me out of tear-swollen eyes, so full of pain and disbelief that a lump came to my throat. "Bob, she's not here. You have to get on with living . . . every moment. That's how anybody survives the bad stuff, me included. Enjoy the now. Enjoy . . . me."

For a moment I couldn't breath. "The now, huh?" I echoed. "I guess that's just it. My now is getting this killer. Everything I've done so far has been for that one purpose."

She swiped at her eyes. "I get it. Harry was there and he was what you needed. I fell into your plan as . . . a good cover. I'm not stupid, Norris. The streets have made me a lot older than my driver's license says. And another thing they taught me. Patience. So stick that in your fat wallet and wash it down with that piss beer you like so much!"

"I hate—"

A solid knock stopped me from saying "that beer." Lori motioned for me to answer the door while she cleaned her face at the sink.

Roy entered the minute I opened the door. "What brings you here?"

"What you said on the phone. It bothered me."

Lori breezed by as we settled at the table. Roy's eyebrows rose in appreciation, but he forgot her as he looked at me.

"What exactly do you have going, Norris?"

Knowing he didn't mean Lori, I outlined my plans for Trout.

He shook his head. "You might have an entrapment set up. We'll have to do this carefully to make it work . . . and stick. I'll tell the judge an informant told me of a possible holdup, but I won't say anything about you planning it. Your name can never be mentioned in this crime."

"That'll be easy. This is Harry's store. I've never even been in this one. But, once Trout's arrested, how are you going to keep him quiet. He'll want to point fingers, won't he?"

"One step at a time. There are ways." He stood up and unbuttoned his shirt.

"What the hell—"

"My bullet-proof vest." Velcro rasped apart and he shrugged out of the heavy protection. He laid it on the table and put his shirt back on. "Harry should wear it."

"And you?"

"I've got an extra stashed under my spare tire. That tire covers a lot of police junk. Right handy."

I followed him to the Ford Taurus parked in the alley entrance, as if ready for a get away. Once we hit the street, he went into a comparison of grades of Marijuana. I nodded a lot. After opening his trunk, he positioned me to block the view from the Laundromat across the way. Then he pulled aside the tire and shrugged into the replacement vest. I glimpse a riot helmet, nightstick, and shotgun, as well as a box of rubber gloves. Beat 'em off or shoot off a load, but don't touch 'em without protection. Hm, kind of like the battle between men and women. Lori's image blinked across my mind, but Roy conveniently changed his subject so I had something else to think about.

"You got anything else to do this afternoon?"

"I'm without a car, so I guess not. Why?"

"Want to ride with me? Might do my reputation some good to have Picasso at my side."

"Sounds interesting. Why not!"

"Wait a minute. You ride with me, as in stay in the car whenever I get out to talk to anybody. You only get out when invited. Understand?"

We visited several bars. I went inside at each one, Roy holding the door for me, like I was somebody special, which was exactly the impression he wanted. He ordered beer, but always toyed with it, instead of drinking. He cautioned me to do the same. Since none of the places carried the imports, it was easy to follow his lead.

The man's eyes constantly moved, looking over people, dark corners, movement, traffic, store fronts and sidewalks. Three times he escorted me to the car then returned to the bar to talk to some scuzzy informant, usually in the bathroom.

In the last bar, I caught the reflection of the slanting sun on the glass door as it opened.   My watch said 6:20. I tugged on Roy's sleeve to get his attention. He leaned toward me.

"Trout will be at the Stop-and-Go in fifteen minutes."

"Let's get moving."

We parked across the street. I reached for the door handle.

"Stay in the car, asshole. That's Trout's van half-way down the block, isn't it?"

I stared at the vehicle and suddenly remembered seeing it across the street from the Stop-and-Go where Eileen died. This time it blocked an alley and sat empty, no shadowy figures waiting. My heart began to thunder.

Roy had his binoculars out. "Trout's at the coolers. Long raincoat on, probably covering that shotgun of his. There's one, two customers. He's watching them. Looks nervous. One's paying. The other is stepping up. There. He's paid and is coming out the door. Trout is easing up toward the counter."

I couldn't understand why he sounded so calm and mater-of-fact, while I felt ready to jump out of my skin.

"I'll let him get the money, then I'll move in. You stay here and watch. If Trout shoots or doesn't drop to the ground when I yell, you call for back-up."

"What? Me?"

He dropped the binoculars, pulled the radio from under the dash, and shoved it in my hands.

"Push this button."

"What do I say?"

"Help. Then say 'Frank sixteen,' release the button, and listen for an answer. Keep it up until you get the dispatcher's return."

"'Help.' I can do that."

He pulled the biggest gun I had ever seen from under his denim vest. Desert Eagle. That's what Harry had called it. It looked expensive and deadly. Roy opened his door and dropped to a crouch.

I fumbled with the binoculars, but finally got them focused on the check-out counter. Trout stood in front of it, the shotgun propped on his hip. Harry placed several bank pouches into a large grocery bag sitting on the counter.

My heart climbed into my throat as Trout scooped the bag in one arm and brandished the shotgun with the other. He backed to the glass doors then charge through. I swept the tight area looking for Roy. He stood pressed to the rear of the van. Unawares, Trout ran toward him.

"Stop! Police!"

My brain shifted into slow-motion. Trout swung the shotgun barrel up. A firecracker popped, immediately followed by a cannon boom. Trout flew backwards then flopped to the ground, motionless. Roy walked passed the side of the van, his Desert Eagle still aimed at Trout.

My shaking hand gripped the radio. I pressed the button, startled at the loud click. Roy had said "If he shoots or doesn't hit the ground." Since both had happened, I released the button. Better that Roy make the call. He didn't want my name involved and neither did I.

Harry ran up to Roy and pounded him on the back. My stomach rolled.

Chapter Thirteen

Harry came out of his bedroom earlier than Lori and I expected. A coffee mug swung carelessly from his fingertips. He set it on the table for Lori to fill before sitting down himself. I eyed the cup. It had a V.F.W. emblem on the side.

"Didn't know you were a joiner." I indicated the cup.

"I ain't. They were handing them out at the hospital yesterday."

Dressed in that football jersey she favored, Lori wiggled into a chair, pulled her knees up, set her chin on her knees, and stared at Harry with big, expectant eyes. She looked like a little girl ready for a storyteller to open a book. When Harry didn't seem ready to spill his guts, she prodded him. "So, you didn't have to work the night shift?"

"Nope. The cops finished by ten, but the district supervisor had me lock up at midnight, kind of like getting the night off for doing a good job."

"Well, you didn't . . ." I stammered. "Roy was the one—"

"Not that. Supervisor didn't care about the shooting. He was just glad he didn't have to use the money he brought to re-open the store." A grin twitched around his lips as he played with us.

"Trout didn't take it all?"

For a moment his eyes narrowed at me. "What Trout took the cops claimed as evidence, just like I thought they would. So, I made sure Trout didn't take any of my goddamn money."

"Harry!" Lori pouted. "Will you cut it out and just tell us what happened. Bob was there. I wasn't. I got a right, ya know! I, ah, I made sure you put on that friggin' vest, didn't I?"

He raised his hand to quiet her.

"I found this big box of play money in the stock room. Supposed to use it for some advertising thing coming up. I just took the real money out of each store's pouch and put that in the safe. The play money went in the pouches. Damn cops wanted to know how I knew to do that. I told 'em I had been held up a while back and I wasn't about to let any sonofabitch get a dime off me again. Too much at stake this time. A hunch, I called it. I had one hellaciously happy boss, I can tell you that!"

He grinned at Lori. I thought for a minute she was going to clap her hands in delight. Bouncing in the chair was bad enough, with that jersey and no bra. I shook my head to get back to Harry.

"So you came off a hero. I'm glad."

"No thanks to you, but I guess Roy saved us all a big hassle."

"That's not why he shot Trout. It was self-defense."

"If it makes you happy, you go right ahead and believe that."

I glanced from him to Lori and back. "He wouldn't . . . I mean, I saw it. You saw it."

"Yep. Damn clean shot. Good aim. Deliberate like."

I shivered. Deliberate. And you set it up, Norris.

"On a brighter note, guys, I got a job at Bison, in the mail room," Lori interjected.

Like two disbelieving idiots, we stared at her. Her happy expression turned defensive.

"It was the clothes. And that clean make-up crap. All right? I looked like some fresh-faced, All-American girl and they hired me. Since I had no job references, the mail room was all I could get. Shut your mouths! You're both catching flies!"

"No, no, Lori! That's great. Really." I tried to cover up my male stupidity. "When do you start?"

"Monday morning. And I found out about Bill Turner. He's not real popular. Kinda the company asshole. Eileen never mentioned him?"

"She didn't bring the company business home, just like I didn't talk school. I think she said more in that last car ride . . ." I hesitated as the painful memory shot through me. Looking up into Lori's understanding gaze, I regrouped and continued. "She talked about her suspicions and that she had to make that call. No, she never mentioned Turner and didn't recognize him, I . . . don't think."

"He was wearing a mask and it all happened so quick. She never knew . . . Well, you know," Harry tried to reassure me once again.

"Yeah, she didn't know him, but now . . . I do." My finger tip traced the rim of my cup as I thought over some alternatives for her killer. Harry had talked about using explosives in Nam. No, that would be too quick. Turner had to suffer, slow, screaming—

"Yo! Bob!" Harry finally got my attention. "Let me repeat what I just said and only Lori heard. I don't think Turner really wanted to pull that trigger."

"What? You were there! You saw the bastard—"

"Yes, I did and he was shaking like a leaf. At first he aimed low, like he meant to avoid a fatal shot. But she moved and he shook. The round went high. That instant I looked at his eyes. They were wide, horrified. He'd never shot anybody before and he didn't like what he'd done, maybe what he'd been paid or forced to do."

"You're trying to make me feel sorry for him?" I almost yelled.

"No! He had the choice and he made it. He did it. Period. I'm just saying there's more to this whole thing and that's what you need to go after . . . not just Turner."

I rubbed my forehead. "Maybe we should just call the police with all this."

"No!" Harry didn't even hesitate. "Who would it be turned over to? Morten! Who would that dumb sonofabitch talk to first? The brass at Bison. Didn't that Maggie say the whole bunch of 'em were tight? That means, if Harper is involved in any way . . . it would blow everything. He'd cover his tracks and be outta here before anyone could take another breath. As popular as you are with Ol' Henry, he'd probably turn around and accuse you!"

Lori nodded her agreement.

"What about Roy?"

"I don't trust him."

"He helped us with Trout."

"You mean took him out for us. Real considerate of him."

My fingers drummed on the table in exasperation. Harry and Lori waited quietly while my brain tried to put things in order.

"Okay, here's the deal. Lori goes to work Monday, looking for as much information as possible on Turner and Harper. Maybe, through her, we can get one of them talking and set up a tape or video."

Harry tilted his chair back on two legs, grinning at me. "Sounds good but . . . I'd rather go in blasting everyone with guns."

I grinned back. "Yeah, me, too."

"Men!" Lori rolled her eyes.

I parked right in front of Bison's "No Parking" sign. Lori smiled at me. Really smiled. "Thanks for the lift. If you had bought me a car, instead of that Mustang for Harry, you could have slept another half hour."

I shrugged. "Buy a car or sleep? Which can I afford?"

Her smile turned into a grin and those calf-eyes of hers snapped with playful delight. She looked good enough to . . . ogle, wearing a new Leanne Dorf outfit from Marci's. The matching vest and fitted slacks looked perfect with the soft leather flats covering her painted toe nails. For a moment I worried that she might look too good for the mail room, but dismissed that. She looked damn good for her first day and that was her intention.

As she slid out of the car, I called, "Have a good one!"

She saluted me with a thumbs up then slipped into a crowd of office girls going through the front doors. A sudden emptiness hollowed my chest. I fought it by whipping out into traffic. A horn blared. I waved the finger out the window and started weaving in and out of traffic, in a hurry to get someplace, but not knowing where.

My attention wandered, drifting back to Bison, envisioning where Lori would be, what she would be seeing, what she would be doing. For a second I wondered if she saw this Bison opportunity like Harry did the Stop-and-Go, a real job in the middle of this mess, something that would go on when my mission was accomplished.

A masked faced flashed across my memory, Turner's masked face. He's behind you at Bison. I slammed on my brakes, ignoring the sound of screeching tires and yelling. Two seconds later, traffic in the opposite direction opened up. I swung the little car around and headed back, glad no cop car had seen all the laws I just broke. I didn't have time for that right now. My mind could only handle one thing: Find out why Turner killed Eileen.

Taking Bison's private drive, I went around the building to the management parking lot. It didn't take long to locate the space reserved for "B. Turner, Building Security." It was empty, so I filled it with my Ferrari.

Thirty minutes of the Neil Diamond tape played before I heard the car horn. In the mirror, a large white Ford blocked my exit. The driver's door opened. Giorgio Italian shoes stepped to the pavement, probably the same ones he had worn at the robbery.

Turner stopped at my door and tapped on the window. I pushed the switch allowing the glass to slide noiselessly into the door panel. Pasting a Henry-type smile on, I looked up into his stone-chiseled face and politely asked "May I help you?"

He stared at me in disbelief. "What do you mean 'May I help you?' Can't you read the goddamn sign in front of you?"

I turned my head a moment as if noticing the sign for the first time, while my brain went into the Harry-prepared mode. ". . . And you are B. Turner?"

"Yeah. Who the hell are you, Mr. Hotshot-in-a-fuckin'-Ferrari?"

"Bob Norris."

He started to say something, blinked, then took a step backwards. His head swiveled as he took it the absence of people in the lot, then his gaze swept the office building windows for any observers. His right hand slid under the front flap of his Stafford suit jacket and the next instant I stared down the barrel of a chrome revolver. Strangely, I felt very calm, even in control.

"Get your ass out of that car right now!" His voice quivered. A good sign.

"Are you going to shoot me if I don't?"

"Are you going to sit there and find out?"

"I'm sure you don't want a dead man sitting in your parking space."

He lowered the gun. Harry was right. I saw it in Turner's eyes. He had no taste for pulling a trigger. Even if ordered. I had to know who was issuing those orders.

The revolver slowly disappeared back into its shoulder holster. The next moment the Mason ring on his right fist came at me. The fist felt like a wrecking ball exploding into my face and everything went black.

The blackness lightened into a throbbing white light behind my eyelids. A high-pitched ringing bounced around inside my head. I tried to bring a hand up to rub my face, but couldn't. That's when I tried to open my eyes. Nausea rose. I swallowed several times, working to get a grip on that white light. Finally, I managed to crack one eyelid. The left one throbbed and wouldn't budge.

Swollen shut. Fist. Mason Ring. Turner.

My limited sight grew hazy as I tried to look around. Damn! My head felt hollow and heavy, as if twice its size. Again I tried to touch it, but realized my hands had been bound behind me. Someone, Turner probably, had set me on a cement floor against a brick wall in a large, shadowy room. I was alone.

Fighting the pain and sick feeling, I looked up. High above me, a small window admitted the only light. Dust particles floated in the shaft of bright sunlight. The musty smell of the place told me it had not been used lately. Warehouse. A light area on a far wall looked like some sort of door. Thirty yards of squirming would get me to it, but I knew that would be a worthless effort. Turner would have secured it from the other side, unless he was fool. He hit me rather than shoot me. He was no fool.

I moved my fingers, discovering my wrists had been taped together. Wide tape, probably goddamn duct tape. I had always hated the stuff and now wished I could strangle its inventor. I strained that one good eye trying to see into the shadows, looking for something, anything sharp that might have been thrown aside or left behind. A piece of glass kicked into a corner would be nice. The dim light and the pain limited my field of vision.

When I tried to move my legs, I found the bastard had taped my ankles together, too. Rolling onto my side made my head pound worse and pushed my nose into the dusty floor. I inhaled the sour smell of mouse droppings. The sneeze just about exploded my head.

I fought the curtain of blackness that tried again to suffocate me. Steel rubbing on steel echoed across the warehouse. I forced myself to stay awake.

The door opened and Turner entered. He stood a moment, his head turned in my direction. I guessed his eyes were adjusting to the dimness.

"Fell over, did you? Is that more comfortable, Norris?"

When I didn't answer, he walked closer, until his Giorgio shoes once again filled my vision.

"Hey, I'm talking to you!" The shoe landed solidly in my ribs. I curled, fighting blackness and pain. Air! Take a breath. When I gasped, I heard his laugh.

"Mean . . . son . . . of . . . a . . . bitch," I whispered.

Squatting on his heels, he peered hard at me. His grin showed off perfect teeth. Probably capped. Right next to breathing was the need to break those caps.

"This is going to be your luxury suite . . . until the Skipper tells me what to do with you. Is the little man hungry?"

"Oh, yeah," I muttered. "Bring me . . . a burger and fries."

"There ya go. The proof that you've really come down in the world. Lost your appetite for expensive beef and French shit?"

I hawked and spat at him. His hand flashed out, but he only twisted my shirt front. Reluctantly he slammed me back to the floor. I swallowed the grunt of pain.

"You mind your fancy manners, or I won't feed you anything but the rat shit in this place."

"What would . . . this 'Skipper' say?"

"I wouldn't tell him, would I?"

"Who is he?"

Turner chuckled without humor. "You don't need to know and you're never gonna know."

"Is he why you . . . didn't kill me?"

"He calls the shots. Get it? Shots?" He tapped a vicious finger against my forehead. "Right there. He gives the word and the bullet will splatter your goddamn brains all over this brick wall."

"A quick end. Better than . . . I had planned for you."

He flicked his finger against my forehead, grinning when I flinched. "How did you find out I killed your wife?"

"An admission of guilt. Not too smart."

"Oh, like you're gonna tell somebody. Answer the goddamn question!"

"I followed . . . the smell of your shit!"

"I'd kick you again, but I want you to tell me who else knows."

Though it hurt like hell, I slowly shook my head, then asked "Why did Harper want my wife dead?"

"Who? Harper, the big-shot Vice President? He got canned yesterday for ripping off five hundred grand from the company. That fancy Ferrari of yours must not have a radio. It's all over the news that the cops arrested him for knocking off his wife."

Why did he look so smug telling me all this? I closed my one eye and tried to think. Harry's theory and my own conclusions had just been flushed down the toilet.

Blocking everything but the need to sit up, I collected myself and jerked upright. When I opened my eye, I saw a glint of admiration in Turner's eyes.

"Since I'm dead . . . anyway," I panted, "tell me who wanted Eileen dead."

"Naw, I don't think so. I don't like you. I wouldn't tell you anything . . . even as you took that last breath." Squatting in front of me, he rocked as he laughed hard at his own sick joke.

In the outline of the light from the open door, I saw the flash of a human form running, jumping. The collision against the unsuspecting Turner sent him rolling. A pink-trousered leg whipped across my vision. Turner's head snapped back and he somersaulted, thudding against the wall. He lay motionless.

I moved my eye this way and that, dazed and not quite believing Lori knelt before me, tugging at the tape on my wrists.

"How . . . " I started to ask.

She pulled out her blouse, bit at an edge until a piece ripped free. Folding that into a pad, she carefully dabbed at the dirt and crusted blood at my left eye. "Goddamn, you look like hell! If he really hurt this eye, I'll kill the bastard myself."

"You got a . . . good start."

She gave me a quick smile and quicker shrug. "I told you the streets taught me a thing or two. Now shut up . . ." Her fingers tore at the tape on my ankles. "We gotta get you to a hospital."

"Just get me to my feet. I'll be all right."

"You sit right there. I knocked a phone out of Turner's pocket. I'll use that."

I watched her search the floor. "How did you know . . . where to find me?"

"Went outside for a smoke. Heard your goddamn car alarm. Nothing sounds like that alarm, Norris. I caught a glimpse of you slumped over in this asshole's car as he drove by. Since I still had your car keys from the other day, I just jumped in and followed him. He lost me, though, and I had to drive around the warehouse district. Where is that friggin' phone?"

She jubilantly scooped it up, punched in numbers, then gave the address.

"I must have bumped the alarm trigger when he pulled me out. How did you find this place?"

"Would you believe I found Turner's car parked next to that couch we dumped Alabama on? Down the way was this door busted open."

She again knelt before me to blot the blood that trickled from my eye and cheek. Grimacing away from her, I froze, then whispered, "Turner's right behind you. With a gun."

She spun up, legs flashing. The gun flew through the air and clattered onto the cement floor. Totally surprised, Turner backed two big steps, then ran through the open door.

"Good. Real good. You, ah, didn't learn that . . . on the streets."

Like she searched for the phone, she now searched for the weapon.

"Classes at the Y. Right after I started whoring."

I heard the annoying siren of an approaching ambulance. Then I made the mistake of trying to use one hand on the brick wall to pull myself to my feet.

Lori saying "Shit!" was the last thing I heard as the blackness returned.

I squirmed under the crisp, clean sheets and knew immediately I was not waking up in my own bed. Opening my right eye to blurred images, I confirmed it. I was in a hospital bed. Two figures took shape nearby. I listened to their whispers. Harry and Lori. Since my tongue really did feel stuck to the roof of my mouth, I got their attention by clearing my throat.

Lori immediately hovered over me, her cool hand stroking the unhurt side of my face. "Quiet. The nurse will be here in a minute. Had us worried. You've been out for two days!"

I wanted to tell her that word was the last thing I heard before passing out, but couldn't work up the energy to be entertaining. Two days! Then I remembered her saying "If he really hurt this eye, I'll kill the bastard myself!" Instead of laughing over that, I sighed, drifting, feeling lighter as if a wind carried me up like a kite. Sunlight and colors. Yeah, I need to see to paint. That's what I am, an artist. Aren't I?

I settled gently down, down. Not falling, but like a feather, until the wind lifted away and I sat in a rowboat. At the stern, Eileen sat in front of me, silent, patiently waiting. She smiled. I took up the oars and began to row, not randomly, around and around, but in one direction. I set the oars deeper, pulled harder. My arm muscles ached as I pulled against the current. The gentle breeze roared into a high wind. Faster and faster the oars hit the water. The distant shore rose and swirled into the darkening clouds overhead until a giant twister formed. I looked to see if Eileen was worried that I might not get us away from that storm. She had disappeared. I was alone in the boat. Above me, the sky lightened until all was blue and clear.

Both my eyes opened on the bright sunlight slanting past the colorful hospital curtains.

"Hello, Mr. Norris. Can you hear me?"

I blinked, my left eyelid moving a little slower than the right. The blurred lines and forms in the room grew more distinct, more vivid. A young nurse stood beside me, watchful, friendly. I swallowed then tried to wet my dry lips with my drier tongue. She gave me an ice chip. I sucked on the piece of heaven.

"Where-where's Harry and Lori?" I finally rasped out, not sounding like myself.

"They went home hours ago. Here's a whole cup of ice. I'll hold it. You just sip."

"What happened?"

A frown brushed over her face, then she gave me an encouraging smile. "The doctor will be here shortly. You suffered a concussion and a small hemorrhage into your left eye. But everything is clearing up nicely."

I closed my right eye. The vision from the left was a bit blurry, but there. She smiled at my testing it.

"It'll be normal in a few days."

My hand drifted up to the bandages on my face and head.

"Those will come off shortly. You have some stitches under there. Harry said to tell you the few scars would make you look like him. But he was laughing when he said it. You have nice friends."

I smiled back. "Yeah, I know. Tough, too." Obviously she had drawn her own conclusions about Harry. I decided not to explain the many sides of Lori.

The afternoon passed slowly. I couldn't sleep, probably because I was slept-out. Dr. Burroughs came by. She went into more details than the nurse had, though I only understood half of her medical gibberish. When she listened to my chest and made me take deep breaths, I found out I had two broken ribs. Finally, she happily reported I could be discharged the next morning, after the last of the IV antibiotics and the dressings came off. So I had one more night in the medical prison.

Lori walked in while I feasted on gelatin. Apparently embarrassed by the flowers she brought, she shoved them beside another small arrangement already sitting on my bedside table.

"Flowers?"

"Harry got those down in the gift shop yesterday. He said a pansy-assed art teacher would probably want something more than TV soap operas to look at. I, ah, didn't like what they had. I went to a real florist. So, you look a whole helluva lot better. How're you feeling?"

"Sore. Headache, ribs ache. What happened to Turner? Did the cops arrest him?"

"No," she said fiddling with the ribbon on the flowers. "He claimed self-defense. Said you beat the crap out of him. Didn't want to admit a woman knocked him on his ass. He never got a good look at my face, just my back."

"And your feet . . . as they hit him."

She tried not to grin. "More like my shoes. I'm still working at Bison and actually see the bastard every day. I'm sure he doesn't know me."

"Didn't the cops question you? Didn't you tell them what happened?"

"Well, I . . . not everything. The cops and ambulance arrived. I told them I was passing by the alley when I heard a fight going on. I told them you gave your name and Turner's before passing out. Before they could ask for my driver's license or anything, I split. Remember I've still got a warrant hanging over my head?"

"Oh, sorry. I-I forgot. So . . . much . . . going on." I felt my life on the end of a rope dangling over a deep canyon, one hand slipping, the other getting tired. I lay in a bed of a public hospital anyone could get into. One quick slice and that rope would be cut. Turner knew I knew. He didn't like pulling a trigger, but I had pushed him into a corner. And who the hell was his "Skipper?" What was that man capable of?

"Lori, is there a guard on my door?"

"Guard? Lots of nurses and staff running all over, but nobody has been like assigned to just you."

"Turner admitted he killed Eileen, but only because he thought I was a dead man already. He talked about orders from somebody he called 'Skipper.' There's two people who seriously want me dead."

"You're right!" She began to pace around the foot of the bed and back, something I had never seen before. Her worry only increased mine. "Maybe he hasn't tried anything because either Harry or me has been here these last three days, like in shifts. He was here when I worked and I came in and sat through the night."

My heart clenched with that explanation. Tears burned at my eyes. No one in my entire life had paid that kind of attention or worried that much about whether I lived or died. Don't make a pansy-assed fool of yourself and cry, Norris! I cleared my throat and clenched my jaw, even though that made my face and head hurt.

"Except for this entire afternoon. I've been awake and no Harry."

She fidgeted then finally said, "Well, he kinda wore himself out and you know how he is. I mean it's not like he could help it. He had a flashback at work last night, right in the middle of the Stop-and-Go, with customers watching and everything. The cops called an ambulance. He just got out of VA hospital about an hour ago and called me. They put him on some new stuff, stronger, I think."

I closed my eyes and pressed myself into the bed. That wouldn't have happened without all this. Here he is getting worse because of me. And you! You're fighting a man twice your size because of me! And here I am, a friggin' punching bag, flat on my back."

"Sounds like you're feeling sorry for yourself, Norris."

"All I've done is get you two into trouble and all because of my trouble. I've screwed up your lives every time I turned around."

"Right. Like Harry and I didn't have a choice. Grow up, Norris! Take responsibility for yourself! Do something!"

I glared at her. "Now you're sounding like Henry!"

"Hey, you think maybe once in a while the old man was right? How'd he get to be so rich? By being wrong?"

"Ha, ha! You are so funny. Well, I'll do something, all right. Tell Harry to buy me some ammo for that stolen gun he gave me. I've got plans for the minute I leave this place."

"I'm not so sure you're up to any rough stuff."

"Who asked you? I don't need your permission. In fact, I'm ready to test all your street lectures. What do you think of that?"

She shook her head in total disbelief. "I don't think its funny . . . that's what I think."

Chapter Fourteen

My eyes snapped open on the semi-dark hospital room. The little machine that ran the IV's stood beside the bed, its low humming and pumping silent since my IV had been taken out. Carefully, I touched my face. The bandages had been removed, too, and the pain was less. No, just moving hadn't awakened me. Something else.

The bathroom door stood open a couple of inches, providing the only light in the room. Lori slept like a kitten, curled in the cushioned chair. Whatever it was hadn't awakened her. Of course, working days and sleeping nights like that, she had to be exhausted. Maybe a fire alarm would wake her up. Maybe.

The door to the hallway moved slowly inward. I glanced at the clock. Only twenty minutes ago, the nurse had taken my vitals then whispered I wouldn't be bothered the rest of the night. Tension swept over me.

For three days I had been a target, unconscious and available in that bed. Since talking about it with Lori, even the slightest sound had me ready to defend myself. I refused to be a victim a second time. Rehearsing my moves in such limited space had kept my mind busy. Lori challenged me to do something, hadn't she? If this was it, I hoped to hell I wouldn't freeze up.

A figure in dark clothes slipped quietly into the room, easing the hallway door closed. It clicked into place and I knew what had brought me out of my light sleep.

Under the covers, my hand found the nurse's call button. I gently pushed it down, grateful it made no sound. The figure tiptoed across the carpeted floor then side-stepped behind the privacy curtain pulled half-way between the room's empty bed and mine.

I glanced at Lori. The chair faced the doorway, but her eyes were closed. She slept unawares. I had to act alone. My hand slid over my chest. This goddamn idea of Harry's better work. But, what if he shoots me in the head? Always gotta find something, don't you, Norris?

Forcing my eyelids half-closed, I tried to breathe naturally. Then he was beside me, the bathroom light reflecting off the raised knife. I looked full into Turner's wide eyes as he slammed the blade down. The metal skittered off the bullet-proof vest.

Turner's flicker of surprise turned to determination. I grabbed his wrist with one hand and pulled back the palm with the other. The knife didn't drop like Harry said it would.

The next instant two slender arms criss-crossed his neck and yanked him back. At his shoulder, Lori's face appeared, contorted with her effort to choke the bastard. He jerked forward, pulling her off her feet and onto his back. From deep inside me came the power to smash my fist into his face. Blood sprayed from the corner of his eye, but didn't stop him. In fact, his expression changed to a mad man's, flaring nostrils, gruesome smile showing gritted teeth, pinched, hate-filled eyes. A face I would never forget.

I rolled from the bed as he lunged for me again, Lori still clinging to his neck. She loosened her hold a moment to pull one arm tighter, his throat in the crook of her elbow, his jaw forced out in an opened-mouth gasp. Since his attention had been diverted to her strangle-hold, I jumped onto the bed in a crouch. My powerful right upper cut caught his extended jaw. Bone crunched. I hoped it wasn't my knuckles. His eyes rolled closed and he sagged to his knees. Lori stepped away, letting him fall to the floor.

As she moved, he rolled and came up by the second bed, knife in hand. He sliced the air. She backed. He stepped forward, but she dodged. I was about to leap on his back when she snapped one leg up, sending the knife spinning into the air. One, two kicks to the stomach and he doubled over, backing to the foot of my bed. Desperate for air and gagging, he turned, his hands clawing at his chest. Without hesitation she jumped. Both feet connected with his butt. Like a bulky rocket, he shot across the wall shelf he faced. His head collided with plate glass and it shattered. The bottoms of his Giorgio Italian shoes followed him out the window.

My jaw worked, but no words came out.

"What floor are we on?" Lori gasped as she staggered to her feet.

I slid from the bed to look. "Ah, about the sixth, I guess."

She stepped beside me to look down at the alley. Three street lights cast a yellow haze over everything, yet we could distinctly see the hospital loading dock and stacks of pallets. No body sprawled on the pavement.

I pointed at an enormous dumpster directly below us, its lid propped open. "You think he fell in the trash?"

She shrugged. "At least he had something soft to land on, unless it's full of gross hospital crap. I hope so."

Hearing the hall door open, Lori whipped the window curtains closed. I straightened my hospital gown to cover the vest.

The nurse softly called out, "Mr. Norris? Did you push the call button?" Her pert, concerned face peered around the privacy curtain.

I looked at the clock as I climbed back in bed. "Yeah about five minutes ago. What took you so long?"

"We're short two people tonight. Running our legs off. Really, I got here as quickly as I could. What is it you need?"

I held up my throbbing right hand. It had begun to swell. "I hurt my right hand . . . while I was asleep."

"He had a nightmare," Lori offered.

The nurse's gentle hands and fingers examined me. She mumbled, "I'll have to call the doctor. This needs to be X-rayed."

Moments later, a young aide pushed my wheelchair toward the elevator. Lori walked beside me, trying not to smile. I rolled my eyes at her.

"While, ah, you're in X-ray, I'll go out for a smoke and check out the dumpster."

"Did you lose something, Miss?" the aide asked.

I glared. Lori chewed on her lip then managed, "Window had been cranked open, you know just a couple inches, for fresh air. Something accidentally fell out."

I discovered nothing happened fast in a hospital unless somebody's heart stopped. After waiting forever for the X-rays, I sat in an exam room in the E.R. for someone to wrap my hand. Another hour passed before the aide came with a goddamn wheelchair to take me back to my room. The whole thing took three hours. It didn't matter that my hand was only sprained and bruised. I had to know what Lori found.

Despite the aide's protest, I climbed out of the wheelchair at the doorway and walked into my room. Lori stood nose to nose with a short, fat man wearing tan pants and shirt. His embroidered name patch read "Elmer."

"I don't know how the window got broke. But it looks to me like that goddamn machine fell over. It is half sticking out the friggin' window!"

"I don't have to put up with talk like that, ma'am. I'm just the maintenance man. I have a report to write . . ."

"Well, Mr. Maintenance Man, it looks like you are doing one piss-poor job." Her painted finger nail pointed. "Wheel's missing from the stand. Looks to me like the goddamn thing fell over! You try to blame this on Mr. Norris or me and we'll get a friggin' lawyer to sue for negligence! How do you like that?"

He shifted nervously, glanced at me, then held up his hands in surrender. "I-I, ah, think I'll talk to the nurse. This can't be fixed tonight, so-so she'll have to move him to another room. How's that sound?"

Lori looked at me. I shrugged.

"You do that . . . like pronto!" she ordered.

When he scurried out, she arched her eyebrows and looked smug.

"Pretty good thinking, Lori."

"The little sonofabitch came in here all arrogant-like. I already had it set up, so I wasn't going to let him talk to me like that. I just remembered how you and Henry handled the piss ants of the world."

I held up my hand to quiet her as the aide hustled in the door with that wheelchair again.

Settled in another room, we waited for the aide to leave before talking.

"Did you find Turner?"

"In the dumpster. Not a pretty sight. I think he split his head open, maybe on the edge when he hit. And your hand?"

"Not broken. When will they find the body and put two and two together?"

Her fingers brushed at a soiled spot on her blouse. "I threw a couple pallets on top of him . . . just before a janitor came out to add some more bags. I shared a smoke with him. He said the garbage truck comes around five. When I asked if anyone had to handle all that hospital stuff, he said the container's just lifted and dumped in the truck. Nobody touches a thing or sees a thing. He made it clear he didn't want to, anyway. Turner won't be noticed until he hits the landfill. And the truck makes the rounds of three hospitals, so no one will know where he came from."

As relief took hold, I realized my head, ribs, and hand hurt like hell. Turner is one. There is another.

"But we did him in before finding out about his 'Skipper.'"

She threw herself into the lounge chair. "We? We did it?"

"Hey! I slammed him in the face for you. I did something. Isn't that what you told me to do?"

She cocked her head. "Yeah, I guess I said that. So we'll both take the rap, is that it?"

"I'm depending on no one being able to trace him, but . . . if push comes to shove, yeah, I'll take the blame with you."

Her eyes teared up. She swiped at them then turned business-like again. "Yeah, we gotta search out this 'Skipper' on our own now. Harper is locked up, but he could still be directing things from jail. It has been known to happen."

"Possible, but I don't know. Turner didn't seem to know him. No, I don't think Harper is this 'Skipper.' Yet, everything keeps going back to Bison. Who besides Eileen and Maggie knew what Harper was doing and had ties to Turner?"

"I'm still working there. I wanted to shove that up Ol' Henry's ass but I didn't. I forgot to tell you he called. Well, he left a message on the answering machine the day Turner caught you. We didn't get back to him about all this."

"Don't worry about it. He called the nurse's station yesterday. Got a report on my condition and left the message he couldn't get up to see me. Like I give a damn! The nurse also said he contacted the business office to cover my bill."

"Considerate, ain't he?"

"More like laughing his ass off and thinking I got what I deserved."

That thought made my head hurt worse. I pushed the call button to ask for some pain medicine.

Following my discharge orders to rest, I stretched out on my couch and spent the morning finally reading that old paperback.

On her noon break, Lori called. The Bison employees had been informed of Turner's dismissal the day before and the appointment of Vickie Templeton to replace him. The name sounded familiar to me, then I remembered she was the chick Maggie had said was messing around with Harper. Lori already knew that. Company gossip had it that Harper's arrest had screwed up the woman's ambitions, so she just redirected herself into a role as a department head. She didn't give a damn if it was Security or Cleaning. She just wanted to be top dog someplace. Lori had met her. Her statement "She wouldn't make a good whore!" kind of summarized her opinion.

The rest of the afternoon I kept trying to put the puzzle pieces together. The more I thought about it, the more convinced I was that Turner hadn't been close to Harper, yet he had killed Eileen for investigating Harper. What other reason could there be?

The two o'clock oriental cooking show came on just as Harry wandered across the living room and headed for the kitchen. He reappeared with a glass of orange juice and a handful of pills. After swallowing those, he sat in the arm chair and squinted his eyes at me.

"Morning, Harry," I chirped.

He shivered at my cheerfulness. "Instead of that goddamn TV, you should be listening to the radio. Mine popped on with the news that Turner's body was found at the dump. Kinda gruesome, they said. A worker saw a leg sticking out and pushed aside garbage until he was uncovered. How long's he been there? Two days? Bet he smells pretty bad."

I cleared my throat. "How can you talk like that when you just put something in your stomach?"

"Me? I seen a lot worse in Nam. Dead bodies don't bother me. The assholes walking around? That's another matter."

"Speaking of assholes out there, did you get my ammo?"

He sighed heavily and settled back, studying me as if calculating my readiness. "Loaded and ready for you to commit another murder . . . if that's what you're set on."

"What the hell does that mean?"

"How many people have you seen killed since . . . well, you know?"

"Three. Well, four if you count Chucky and five if you count Maggie, but I didn't see those."

"More than your average bear, I'd say. What does that tell you?"

Unable to hold his gaze, I stared at the muted TV. "Yeah, I'm kinda walking with death, aren't I? An indirect cause, but a cause, all the same."

"Now you're sounding like the reasonable teacher instead of some cartoon avenger."

"Cartoon . . . !"

"Hold it, Lone Ranger. It's not a slam! I'm just saying you need a grip on reality here. The murder tally in this city in the past few weeks passed last year's total. And this year ain't half over! Every one of these people had some connection with Bison or you. Morten may be the world's worse cop, but he ain't entirely stupid."

"Well, he can't tie me to Turner. He was found in the dump!"

"Maybe not Morten, but what about Roy? What's he gonna say when you return his vest with a slice in it?"

"I could say I don't know how it happened."

"He won't buy that! He's not an idiot like Morten. And he knows you were after Turner and that Turner beat you up."

"So where's the proof? Turner didn't exactly have the knife clutched in his death grip . . . 'cause Lori picked it up and jammed it in her purse. We could . . ." I searched for a cover- up. "Yeah, we could drop the vest in the garage, back the car over it, and tell him it got sliced by some glass when it fell out on accident."

Harry shook his head in disgust. "Amateurs! Go ahead, try it. But I want to see you look him in the eye and tell that story."

I slumped. My life of lies was wearing me out.

Abruptly he laughed, without humor. "Just look like that and act confused. You got a friggin' concussion and almost lost an eye! Confusion he'll believe! He has as much faith in your street-smarts as Lori and me, anyway! Quit trying to have all the answers! None of us are that lucky! Just act what you are! Confused!"

I frowned at him. He walked to the kitchen and brought back one of the mild pain pills Dr. Burroughs had prescribed for my first few days home. I downed it with an imported beer chaser, then held up the bottle.

"At least you had enough sympathy to buy me some good stuff!"

He twitched a grin and left me to my TV watching.

Not long after Harry left for work, Lori arrived home with a sack full of Italian carry-out from Pappi's. As the Linguine filled my mouth with rich herbs, garlic, and cheeses, I listened to Lori rattle on about the highs and lows of her day. From the enthusiasm in her face, I could tell she truly enjoyed this "legitimate employment," as Henry would call it.

Like a genie appearing, the phone rang and I listened to his nasal voice.

"Just returned from my trip and found you had been discharged. A very expensive lesson, but worth it, I think, so I shall not take it out of your allowance."

"Damned generous of you."

"You obviously don't believe that or you wouldn't have said it in that tone of voice. Did I, ah, interrupt something?"

"Dinner. Everything Italian tastes better cold, except for their women. But you wouldn't know about that, would you Henry?"

"Another attempt at humor, Robert, that is totally lost on me. I called to tell you of the memorial service for Charles. I'm including Maggie Gates in the service . . . just to expedite things and get on with life, so to speak. Formal invitations are in the mail. Feel free to bring your two friends. Since Charles spoke of them at the hospital and seemed to have some regard for them . . ."

"You mean Lori and Harry?" I asked pointedly.

"Yes, yes. Those two. And please make certain they dress appropriately. There will be some family and business associates who knew at lest one of the deceased. I don't want your present . . . social status, I guess, to upset anyone."

"Your attention to details is . . . just heart-warming, Henry."

"Don't push me, Robert. Do I need to remind you as well to dress appropriately?"

I hung up on him. Lori poured more clam sauce over my drying pasta as I sat down.

"What was that all about?"

"Henry is throwing a going away party for Maggie and Chucky. We get to wear bib-overalls and t-shirts."

She glared at me.

"What? What? You lost your sense of humor now?" I demanded.

"Charles. His names was Charles." She then carefully worked a noodle free, snaked it up to her mouth, and sucked it up. One arched eyebrow challenged me to correct her table manners, then she twisted in her chair. "Hear that?"

"What?"

"That's your friggin' car alarm. I hate that thing. You can hear it two stories up!"

"Hey, because it was annoying it saved my life, right?"

She shrugged. "So, are you going to go see what set it off this time?"

"I suppose. You finish sucking up your noodles."

"No fun without you watching. And besides it gives me gas. I'll go with you. Never know when I might have to rescue you."

"Ha, ha! Another not-so-funny crack!"

The elevator doors opened to the dark, smelly underground garage. The low watt-lighting made it feel like a cave to me. We walked along the line of oil streaks between the twelve numbered parking slots. My Ferrari sat at the end, its alarm echoing off the garage walls and numbing my ear drums. I thumbed the remote. The blessed chirping silenced the alarm.

As I reached for the door handle, my gaze caught the marks where dirt had been smeared across the oil on the pavement at my feet. Someone slid under my car. I wanted to jump away like a man avoiding a striking snake, then realized no one was under there . . . now.

"Do you have a flashlight?"

Lori held her arms straight out from her sides. "Do I look like I would have one? You've got one in the glove box. I'll go around and get it."

"No! Don't touch the car." I pointed at the smears. "Someone's been under it."

Lori knelt and almost laid her cheek against the filth. "Holy crap!" she whispered, then scrambled to her feet and stepped back.

I copied her, staring at the car. "Was I right?"

She nodded. "A box taped there. It has a digital clock. I think we have twelve minutes to do something."

"Twelve minutes?"

"Maybe it's twelve friggin' hours. How do I know? Just don't stand there, Mr. College Man. Do something!"

For some reason I tip-toed back to the car then knelt and looked for myself. Black box, goddamn duct tape, long tube, and a clock. The number twelve glowed in the dark, with the seconds counting down. They read 1-9, so I concluded the twelve meant minutes.

I stood up shaking my head. "Why would someone bomb my car?"

"Who the fuck cares? Give me the keys and I'll drive it out of here before it goes off!"

I clenched the keys to my chest. "You start it and -boom- no twelve minutes. We have to call the police."

"A College Man says this? Haven't you been listening to Harry and me! The police won't get here in time."

I bit my lip and looked around. If it exploded here, the entire building would come down. Probably what was intended, Norris.

"Go open the ramp door then get outside. Run toward the Tickled Pink. I'll start the car and head toward the river. Maybe I can make it there before . . . well, before."

"Bull! I'm going with you."

"No! And there will be no discussion. Get the hell out of here, now! We're wasting time."

A chop of her hand and the keys flew through the air. Before I could even move, she flicked the remote and unlocked the doors. My heart lurched. Nothing happened. Just as she opened the door, I grabbed her arm and swung her away. Again, nothing.

The instant my butt hit the seat, she dived across me and into the passenger seat. As she straightened herself, those wide eyes defied me to kick her out.

"Time's a wastin,'" she quipped.

"Goddamn you, Lori!"

We stared hard into one another's eyes as I keyed the ignition and the motor hummed. Lori punched the garage remote.

"Let's go, Norris!"

Sunlight reflected off the cement valley outside. We stared at that as I hit the accelerator. I prayed if anyone was on the sidewalk they could jump out of the way, because I wasn't stopping for anything. The slow-moving door scraped across the Ferrari's top. Swerving into the street, I worked the clutch and gas like a race driver. Please live up to your reputation, you goddamn Ferrari!

"How many minutes?" I shouted.

"How the hell would I know?" Lori had fastened her seat belt, but one hand still braced against the dash and the other held the door handle.

At the intersection ahead, my light turned red. I didn't slow down.

"Bus! A goddamn bus!" Lori yelled.

I stood on the brake pedal. The little car went into a spin then stopped with a jarring impact. Metal screeched. I blinked at the parked car wrinkled against my window. Lori yanked my hands from the steering wheel then tugged me across the gear shift and out her open passenger door. The fall to my hands and knees on the pavement put my eyes at the same level as the Ferrari's undercarriage. Reality returned. I jumped to my feet, pulling Lori with me. We ran back the way we had come.

"Run! Back! Bomb!" I screamed at the people coming closer to gawk. The panicked crowd scattered.

The instant I heard the explosion half a block behind us, I threw myself over Lori. She grunted as we hit the ground. I twisted to glance back. A large orange ball of fire billowed then drifted up, following its black smoke into the air.

Chapter Fifteen

A week after my Ferrari destroyed two parked cars and made an extra big pothole, I still asked myself why, as well as who. With Turner gone, the options were cut to one. Skipper, whoever the hell that was.

Roy called telling us the cops had chalked up the explosion to the collision, but I wasn't going to be charged with reckless driving. Lori thought that was funny. Then Roy pressed us to move to a safer area of the city and Harry thought that was funny. The three of us decided to stay and face the enemy. It was Roy's turn to laugh.

Harry explained how we could watch one another's backs most of the time. When anyone was alone, the tension was bad. Each day seemed worse. We had to work hard not to bite off one another's head.

Henry sent a "Care" package. Speechless, Lori carried the black crepe dress to her bedroom to try on. She looked incredible and very mature. Harry grunted at his tux, commenting he was surprised Henry didn't send an artificial arm, too. I glared at mine and told them I preferred bib overalls.

The day of the Joint Memorial service Henry's new chauffeur, Peter, knocked at our door at one in the afternoon. Henry insisted we arrive in a style fitting the solemn occasion. I preferred roaring up his pretentious drive in Harry's Mustang.

The young, blond, muscular Peter cautiously drove through the slums then kept to the speed limit on the expressway. Lori kept peering over his shoulder at the speedometer then sighing heavily. Harry tried to strike up a conversation, but Peter stared straight ahead as if his passengers didn't exist. I tried to think of something else, but my thoughts kept going back to the possibility that Peter did more than drive for Henry. I could almost hear Henry say, "How crude, Robert!" Lori kept asking me what I was grinning about, but I wouldn't answer.

The decorative, iron-barred gate opened as Peter swung the limo into the entrance. My friends gawked as we traveled the quarter mile driveway pass tennis courts, a putting green, a miniature lake complete with two swans, and the multi-car garage with a small yacht sitting on its trailer. I pointed out the barn and horse pasture, empty since Eileen's high school days. Henry's three story mansion stood at the crest of a gentle, sloping hill.

I had always hated the place, not because Henry lived there, but because the imported-marble home and the over twenty acres of manicured Kentucky blue grass mocked the working class who stood outside the encircling iron-barred fence and stared in disbelief. Eileen had told me more than once that most of the sprawling homes around her father's had second mortgages and the residents carried more plastic than cash. But not Henry. His fortress was secure from such menial concerns. He prided himself on protecting what was his.

The twisting drive forced the limo to ten-miles an hour, so it seemed to take forever to reach the pink marble steps leading to the mansion's front door. Lori and Harry craned their necks to take in the fountain and statues, the front columns and English ivy. We reached the front steps and, as if by magic, the double door opened. There stood Ben, formally called the House Manager, but a butler any where else. He led the way to the ballroom in the lower level. When my first tour years ago ended in that big open space, I blurted that it looked like a glorified rec room in somebody's over-sized basement. Eileen had laughed; Henry didn't.

Lori and Harry spotted the long buffet table beneath the patio windows. The windows looked out over Henry's backyard or rather his Victorian gardens. I dropped onto an empty sofa and waved to one of the many cute maids, all formally attired in black dresses and tasteful white aprons.

"A beer, please."

"I'm sorry, Mr. Norris," her small squeaky voice announced, "We have only a variety of wines, scotch, bourbon, and gin."

That voice reminded me of her name. "Tina, I know Ben keeps a cold case of beer in the kitchen."

She glanced around, then nodded. "I'll see what I can do."

She returned with a tray carrying a frosted glass, an inch of foam dripping down it's side. Harry and Lori sat down beside me. Lori sipped her punch then balanced her loaded plate of food on her knees. The classic dress, her upswept hair, and the light make-up made her look like any of the other classy women wandering around close to their men. That irritated me, but I didn't hang onto the thought. Harry, too expertly set his plate on his knees then drank from his punch cup. I had seen a few glances his way, usually the eyes honing in on his pinned up sleeve. That annoyed me too, but in a different way. Gonna be a long afternoon, Norris. I decided to just sip my beer so Tina wouldn't have to take another trip to the kitchen. Norris, you still feel like a damn thief sneaking around here! What are you doing here? Pacifying Henry or trying to ease your conscience?

"There's a few guys here that I met before." Lori commented. I tried not choke on the precious beer. "They're pretending they don't know me, probably because their wives are hanging all over them."

Harry choked on the cracker he had just put in his mouth. Since his punch was gone, I offered my beer. He only took a sip then cleared his throat. "Yeah, I've only seen some of these people on TV or in the newspaper. Funny to see them as more than names. Ah, Bob, this is kinda awkward. I mean, okay, we ate, we drank, they're talking, but . . . when's the real thing start? Or is this it?"

"Henry likes his guests to enjoy themselves before he does anything planned, like make speeches or hit them up for money."

"He ain't gonna ask for money is he? At a memorial service?" Lori looked horrified.

"No, no. He does that for charities and politicians, that sort of crap. Eileen never got me to those events, believe me."

Harry snickered. "Yeah, you used to drop by the Stop-and-Go, instead."

"So what will he do here?" Lori asked, daintily wiping her fingers with the napkin. She almost jumped when an attentive maid took the empty plate from her knees.

"The bullshitting is part of socializing, like giving the people time to talk about Chu . . . ah, Charles and Maggie. Henry will make an appearance. He'll tell everyone Charles was a great guy, years of devoted service, that sort of crap. I haven't the foggiest idea what he'll say about Maggie. He didn't even know her!"

Lori frowned. "Then why is he having a memorial for her?"

I shrugged and noticed my beer was just about gone. "She had been Eileen's secretary for several years. Maybe he feels obligated. Hey, you two want to see the house? I can take you on the grand tour."

Another maid whisked the empty beer glass from my hand as I stood.

"That's spooky," Lori whispered.

We walked around several groups of elegant, stone-faced society people, obviously being solemn for the occasion. Harry and Lori resumed their stunned expressions when we found the carpeted, circular staircase. A classic Victorian crystal candelabra hung from the ceiling high overhead. At the top of the stairs, I led them down a long hallway to the library. I thought they would enjoy the floor to ceiling bookshelves. The door was locked.

"It's locked! Henry never locks these doors."

"Can I help you, sir?"

All three of us jumped. Ben stood eyeing us suspiciously.

"Hello, Ben. I was just . . ."

"The services are being held downstairs, sir," he interrupted me.

"I know that. I just thought I would show my friends around."

"That is not permitted today, sir."

"Permitted?" I almost laughed. "Henry won't mind and we won't steal anything." Ben didn't laugh. "Okay, so where is he? I'll ask him myself."

"He is preparing for his guests. Please follow me to the ballroom. He would be most unhappy if you were not there when he speaks."

"That's fine, Ben Boy," Lori piped up, "but where's the little girls' room? I need to powder myself, or whatever you people say when nature calls."

He still didn't crack a smile. "We have a ladies' room downstairs . . . or if you would be more comfortable, there is a servant's bathroom off the kitchen."

I resisted punching him in the nose.

Lori hadn't missed his dig. She batted her eyelashes and assumed her most formal tone. "I'll use the servant's can. Don't want to mess up the guest room. You know how it is after you eat burritos for breakfast. So where is the kitchen. I'm in a hurry."

Ben raised his chin. Harry touched my arm as I stiffened.

Follow this hall to the servants' stairs down to the kitchen. The staff will direct you. Gentlemen? Please follow me."

He did an about face the Marines would have appreciated. Harry and I followed him.

Back in the ballroom, the scene hadn't changed much. I didn't spot Tina, so Harry and I wandered back to the punch bowl.

"Harry, over there by the bar. That tall, balding man. That's Dr. Welsh. Great reputation and Eileen really liked him as a person, too. He might be able to help you with your flashbacks."

Harry gulped his punch. "Heard of him at the VA, but he ain't free and I can't afford what he charges."

I remembered some of Eileen's high praise for the man. "Maybe he'd work something out for you."

Harry lifted his glass as if to warn me.

"No, no. Not charity, just a pro-rated thing. He might even be able to work a deal with someone to get you a good artificial arm."

"I may have my principles, Bob, but I'm not totally brain-damaged. Help, yes. Charity, no. I've gotten along so far."

"Damn it, Harry. I owe you now. You know it. I know it. If I can't get the money, I'll wring it out of Henry. Why should he have all the benefits of his money? Come on. Let's go talk to Welsh."

An exchange of introductions prompted Welsh's recollections of who I was to Henry. We agreed the weather had been fine, then I threw Harry's condition into the conversation. Welsh was immediately interested. He tuned in to Harry's pride and assured him a few minutes of chit-chat was not billable. I piped up that I would stand the bill from that point on. Despite Harry's reluctance, the psychiatrist led him to a corner curved sofa.

Taking up my original spot on a sofa across from the buffet table, I tried not to look bored. The people milling around looked so . . . generic, I couldn't even work up a good idea for a painting. Maybe something moderate, within a post-impressionist, but a touch of Seurat.

As Henry stepped onto the little band platform and began his speech, Lori plopped down beside me. I checked my watch. She had been gone thirty minutes. "Where have you been?"

She gave me that seductive "I-know-something-you-don't" smile that I hated. "Guess what?"

Why not play? "What?"

"You know that maid Tina who got you the beer? Well, I found out her birthday is two days before mine."

"Okay. Where'd you meet her?"

"In the can. She remembered when I was Henry's driver. Anyway, she knows this big secret about Henry. Interested?"

I groaned. "It's not a sex thing, is it?"

"Could be. Why?"

"I don't care, that's why. Just as he is, Henry is enough to make me barf. I can't stomach any more tales about his dark side."

"Oh, no. This you want to hear. About a week or two before Eileen died, Tina heard Ben tell Charles that your wife bought more shares of Henry's business. Did Eileen tell you?"

"Yeah. She thought it would grow her portfolio. I shrugged it off. Her money was her money and we didn't talk about it much."

"What did the two of you talk about?"

"Lots, most of it personal stuff that I'm not telling you. But we had an understanding. She had her job ambitions, I had mine. She had her money, I made mine. Jobs and money were two things we didn't talk about."

"Too bad. Sounds like you should've, this time at least. Eileen bought enough shares to own sixty-one per cent of Ashland Steel. In other words, she took the control away from Henry."

My mind went blank. Why didn't Eileen tell me that? It was obvious why Henry didn't. But, maybe it was just servant gossip.

"Wait a minute. Why would Tina tell you this?"

"She hates Henry and thought you might do something with that information. So are you?"

"Hates him? What's her reason?"

Lori sighed heavily, obviously not wanting to tell more than she had to. "Henry forced her to perform at the Gentleman's Club. I told you the place is into all kinds of perverted crap. They almost killed her one night. Henry has been more or less black-mailing her to keep her quiet and keep her working."

"You think she's telling the truth?"

"I know she is." Lori's eyes glazed with tears. She blinked them away then hurried on. "One more thing is Eileen had a will. Henry made some changes in it before turning it over to his attorney. Seems he threatened the attorney to use that copy for whatever wills need to do."

"That doesn't surprise me."

"But . . ." she sucked in a melodramatic breath, "it's not the original. Tina said the word is that . . . you have that one."

"The only legal-type stuff I have . . . ." My God! "The box. The encrypted files! We gotta get out of here. That sonofabitch got us all here so he knew when to send someone to search the apartment."

"Calm down, Bobby!" Lori patted my arm. "The box ain't there."

"What?"

"While you were in the hospital, Harry took it to a friend, somebody who is a real genius with computers and has equipment coming out his ass. His friend is trying to break the access code."

"Where? Where's this guy?"

"Ask Harry. What's the big rush? You can't do anything with Eileen dead."

"The will, Lori. Eileen must have willed everything to me. That's why Henry is looking for it!"

Her fingers gripped my arm. "You don't think . . . Would he have his own daughter killed?"

I stared into her eyes, the truth bombarding my over-loaded

brain. I heard Henry's voice say "Charles." The sky of my mind cleared. "But what if he found out she wasn't his daughter? What would he feel then? And afterwards . . . he found out about the will and sicced Turner on me. What's he going to do when he finds out I know?" I yanked Lori to her feet. "We really gotta get out of here!"

"Where's Harry?"

"In the corner, talking to the shrink."

"Bob, we don't have a car."

"We'll borrow one of Henry's. Think he'll report I stole it?"

Despite Harry's concentration on something Welsh was saying, he glanced up and caught my motioning toward the patio doors. Everyone in the crowded room, even the servants stood facing Henry, the speech maker. We slipped out the door, across the flagstone patio, and down the steps to the garden sidewalk. I broke into a trot as I led the way around the house toward the garage. Lori muttered a curse before kicking off her high heels so she could keep up.

"Okay, Bob," Harry huffed. "What's up?"

"We're getting out of here. That box your friend has? It may have Eileen's will, too."

"I didn't see anything like that. What's so important we gotta run for it?"

"Henry wants the will."

"Well, he seen us leave. I saw him look at us just as I went through the door."

Panting for breath, we reached the garage. Henry had ten cars in his fleet. Lori pointed to the little Sunbeam. As I scanned the board holding the keys, her hand reached over my shoulder and snagged the limo keys.

"That's not . . ."

"I can drive the limo and it's like a tank. Let's go!"

We piled into the front seat and barely got the door closed before she floored it. The back drive was a straight utility road. She didn't waste time. On our way through, the closing gate almost caught the rear bumper.

"I think Henry's on to us, all right!" she announced as the tires bit into the curb in the turn onto the residential street.   H a r r y and I kept our eyes open and our mouths shut. I didn't want to know if her passing the limo between parked cars on a narrow street at 55 mph was skill or luck.

Harry gritted his teeth at one close call. "Damn it, Lori! Slow down . . . just a little."

"Bob doesn't think Henry's calling the cops. You and I know better. I want to get him as close to that box as possible before I'm caught. If I'm going to jail, I'm going to have a damn good time gettin' there!"

"Getting killed is not my idea of a good time! There's a red light!"

"Too late! We're through it!" I gasped out. "Lori, stop this goddamn thing and let me drive!"

She gripped the wheel harder. "I am not letting the owner of Ashland Steel drive his own car. What the hell is that truck doing?"

Both Harry and I frantically looked around. Brakes squealed, but from the momentum I knew they weren't ours. Harry leaned over. I copied him. Either you are kissing your ass good- bye . . . or this position will save us.

Somewhere outside the car something exploded then steel scraped against steel. A really big horn blared and Lori laughed. My body jammed forward, the dash sliding over my head. I tasted blood. Harry! Gotta see if Harry's hurt! But the collision had locked me under the dash, my head stuck between my knees.

"Harry! Are you okay?" I mumbled.

Inches from my leg I heard "Yeah. Fine. Lori!" he tried to shout. "Can you push the fuckin' seat back?"

Her laughter floated over us again. "Just a second. Just a second. I'm looking for the manual lever. The electrical isn't working."

"What's so goddamn funny?" Harry demanded irritably.

"What? Oh, I missed the truck."

The seat smoothly slid backwards, relieving the pressure. I sat up, staring into Harry's uninjured but angry face. His expression immediately turned to concern. A warm trickle slid down my face and caught on the corner of my mouth.

"You okay? A couple of those stitches popped and you're bleeding a little."

My finger started toward the wound, but his clean handkerchief beat me.

"Does it look okay?" I asked.

"Prettier than mine. Naw, you'll need the stitches replaced is all."

We looked at Lori. She was totally unruffled, probably because she had wisely fastened her seat belt. The windshield had shattered into a spider web so bad we couldn't see out. My door wouldn't open, so we followed Lori out the driver's side. As I stood on solid ground again, I couldn't believe what sat in front of us. She had missed the truck, but buried the limo into the side of a parked police car.

A half dozen witnesses ran toward the accident scene. Harry grabbed Lori and me by the arm and shoved us to the back of the limo.

"You two get out of here. I'll say I was driving."

"You can't do that. I'll take the blame. You and Lori get out of here."

"Yo, Bob you still got beer on your breath and Lori's got a warrant. Get the hell out of here. Now!"

Convinced, we ducked between two untouched parked cars and walked quickly around the corner. I stopped for a peek back. The truck driver who had swerved and run into a traffic pole was climbing out of his cab, his hand pressed to his bloody forehead. Harry was instructing the gawkers to help him.

Behind me, Lori hailed a cab.

"Where are we going?" she asked as we crawled in.

"My house." I gave the driver the address then settled back in the seat to whisper, "I think Eileen put her will in her purse. It was like her to carry something that important, as if she could protect it by just knowing where it was."

"Sounds kinda dumb, but kinda smart, too. I mean, who would carry something really important that any pick pocket could grab."

"A woman who hung her purse around her shoulder and always had one hand on it. She learned that going to college in Chicago."

Lori nodded with admiration. Every once in a while I looked over my shoulder to see if a police car or anyone else followed. Unreasonable as it seemed, I knew Henry was out there somewhere searching.

"I thought you sold your home."

"Real estate company hasn't had one interested buyer."

We sat in silence as the cab turned onto Dodge and headed west.

"You haven't been back since moving to the apartment." Her voice dropped lower. "Will it bother you?"

"I have a specific purpose. It's not like I'm looking for memories, Lori. I know right where that purse is."

She nodded stiffly, as if she didn't quite believe my rationalization.

Twenty minutes after the accident, the cab pulled into the driveway I hadn't seen in weeks. The driver took my last twenty and, for the first time in my life, I was penniless. Self-consciously, I glanced at Lori to see if she had noticed. She was totally absorbed in looking at my former home. I knew she was comparing it as obviously something more than the apartment, but less than Henry's mansion. The thought didn't bother me. Why is that, Bob? Maybe because you've let go of it?

She started toward the house.

"No, Lori. This way." I pointed toward the door that led into the garage where the good Judge Williams had parked my Ferrari Boxer.

I flicked on the garage light. A coating of dust dulled the Boxer's color.

"Hm, Norris, you have a thing for red cars, don't you!"

I shrugged and approached the passenger door. My stomach quivered. I took a deep breath to quiet it.

"I thought you said you needed to get her purse. So . . . she kept it in the car?" Lori couldn't keep the disbelief from her voice.

Through the tinted window I could see every detail of the car's interior. In my mind's eye I could almost see Eileen's form sitting in there, waiting for me to be the gentleman and open the door. "No," I whispered, "she left it there. I-I opened it once, looking for that access code for Maggie, but I left it. Under the seat, right where

Eileen wanted it."

Quickly I unlocked the door, held my breath for fear of inhaling her long-gone perfume, and pulled out the black leather bag.

"Here it is." My statement sounded flat, almost reverent, which was stupid. I cleared my throat and clenched my jaw, forcing myself to the business at hand.

"Do you want me to look, Bob?" Lori asked gently.

I glanced back through the tinted window. Not one hint of Eileen tricked my eyes. "No. She left the boat and she's left the car. She's letting me get on with it."

"What? You're not making any sense."

I waved a hand at her then carried the purse to the wooden bench with its clean and shiny tool box I had never touched. The tools were a "just-in-case" gift from Eileen one Christmas. A laughable gift because we both knew I was as mechanically challenged as I was technically phobic. I had always been and would always be an artist, not a blue-collar type. With a confident smile, I opened the expensive clutch and pulled at the fabric liner that provided a slim, nearly invisible compartment. I tugged the folded document from its hiding place. The print was small, compact, typically Eileen.

"What does it say, Bob?"

After skimming the legal introductions on the first page, the second page gave me shivers that soon settled into cold determination. Eileen had specified I inherit everything, her complete fortune with all accounts listed, as well as her shares in each of her business interests, also listed. Her signature was dark, definitive, deliberate. She had meant this to be.

I lifted my eyebrows at Lori. "You're right. I own the controlling share of Ashland Steel."

"That's good . . . I think. So, ah, what now, boss?"

"I'll find an attorney, a new attorney I think. Someone totally unrelated to Henry in any way, somebody who would relish suing the bastard."

"Well, you better hurry before he gets his hands on that will and has you killed."

"I can find somebody. One court order and the cops will be after him and protecting me."

"Really? The cops have been that helpful to you?"

"Well . . ." My confidence faded.

"Eileen, Alabama, Charles, Maggie, Turner beating you up, that damn bomb that aged me twenty years. Why haven't they been digging harder? What . . . or who is keeping them off? This is one street-smart . . . woman who thinks if you want Henry, you gotta get a confession out of him yourself."

"Oh, yeah, like the man sitting on the throne of power is going to spill his guts to me like Turner did? You said it yourself, Lori. The man didn't get all his money by being stupid. Now, I just have to figure out how to be one step ahead, one thought smarter . . . or more unpredictable."

Chapter Sixteen

With a twinge of apprehension, I crawled behind the wheel of the Boxer. The garage door opener rumbled as Lori settled into the passenger seat. For a moment more I waited. Everything felt normal. I filled my lungs, but no "France's Amour." Instead I breathed in the light floral scent I now identified with Lori. Eileen had left the boat and the car. Now I could see beyond finding her killer. My life could go on, not because I realized I had money, but because I cared where I rowed my boat . . . right after I made Henry pay for what he had done to us piss ants of the world.

"Something wrong?" Lori asked.

"Nope. Something's right." I started the little car and backed out the drive way.

Lori eyed me suspiciously. "You're beginning to worry me again, Bob. You're not making sense."

"I'll explain it someday," I said, watching the garage door close again.

Minutes later, I pulled the Boxer next to Harry's Mustang. Lori and I stared at it a moment.

"What are you going to do about Harry?"

"Probably ask Roy to get him out of jail."

"Hey, it was the truck or the cop car. We're alive ain't we?"

Lori's smart-assed expression disappeared as I gave her my best teacher-warning look.

Opening the door to the apartment I expected to find it destroyed. Instead I found it neat and clean with Harry drinking coffee at the dining room table.

"What the hell took you guys so long?" he demanded.

"What are you . . . How did you . . . How long have you been here?"

"About a half hour."

"Did you clean up the place?"

"No. Why?"

"I thought for sure Henry would have sent someone to search it. So what happened at the accident? What did the cops do?"

"They took me in, of course. Henry refused to press charges for car theft . . . just like you said. I got a ticket for reckless driving. Oh, and I just found out something. Guess who owns this building?"

Harry's guessing games were as bad as Lori's. "Okay, who?"

"Your brother Donald."

"You're kiddin' me." I sat down at the table. "Who told you that?"

"He did. He called. I just finished talking to him a minute before you came. Oh, and guess who's the new building super?"

I shook my head.

He grinned at Lori. "Yup, me."

"Back up, Harry. Did Donald say how he got to be the owner?"

"Henry sold it to him. Something about a tax cut. Anyway, this pays more, so I'm quitting the Stop-and-Go. I hated those hours, anyway."

Lori shoved a cold beer into my hand. Thankfully it was my import brand and not the lousy Pabst she gave Harry.

"Something about this makes me uneasy. Did Donald say anything about me?"

"You betcha. He said 'Tell my brother he's being evicted.' So . . ." He shrugged. "Consider this your first notice, I guess."

My mouth dropped open. Lori looked like she was going to hit him on the head with the beer in her hand. Harry's solemn expression melted into a grin then guffawing laughter. Lori rolled her eyes.

"You're a jerk!" she said as she punched him in the shoulder. "So, what did you say to good ol' Donald?"

"Nothing. I just listened. Since I didn't argue with him I guess he figures I'll do it. Let's see. He said to tell you to get that place at Crazy Horse Lake within two weeks or we'll all be evicted."

"I don't get it," I rolled the beer between my palms. "Why is he doing this?"

"He said he was tired of you playing games and, now, he has the means to make you do something useful."

"Bob, I thought your family didn't have a lot of money. How did your brother come up with enough to buy this?" Lori asked. "I mean, it is a dump . . . in the middle of a lot of dumps. But, from what you've said he's just a working guy. Right?"

"Yeah, though he's a real tight wad. Always saving. He asked Eileen for a couple investment tips over the years. But buy a run-down apartment building?"

"Just to get you to move?" Lori stressed. "But, Bob, don't you think it says something that Henry sold it to him?"

"I know Donald and Henry have been talking. I'm suppose to believe they were both worried about my mental status. Now, we know better about Henry . . . . He's probably manipulating my own brother to get at me every way he can!"

"That couldn't happen in a few hours, Bob. Donald said he just got the final papers."

"Remember when I showed you the notice on our door?"

"What the hell is Henry planning?" I muttered.

Harry gulped the last of his Pabst. "I think he convinced good ol' Donald you shouldn't be living here with us, that's for sure."

"Why?" I looked at Harry and Lori.

"Because we'll influence you somehow?" Harry offered.

"Because he doesn't want the uppity-ups to connect you, his son-in-law, with piss ants like us?"

"Or maybe he's afraid of you."

They both looked at me like I was crazy. I picked up the phone and dialed Donald's office. His secretary immediately connected us.

"Hello, Bob. I'm guessing you received my message."

"Yeah. So, you own my home here. Why?"

"Price was right and it will provide a nice income. Does it bother you that I'm your landlord?"

"Bullshit, Donald. You won't make money on this place. Eight low-rent apartments and only three occupied. The rest are being remodeled. That means money being thrown down the toilet and not being earned back for some time. You just flushed your money away. How much did Henry take you for?"

"Ah, Harry told you."

"Of course. So, how much?"

"Cheap. He wanted to unload it."

"He wanted to involve you. You haven't listened to me over the years, have you? He's worse than a ruthless businessman. He hired someone to kill Eileen."

"You . . . have really gone off the deep end!"

"Listen. He found out she wasn't really his daughter and that she bought Ashland Steel right out from under him."

"Total bullshit! He has a position in that city. He's even respected here in Chicago. Where did you come up with this fairy tale? From those street people you're living with? Have they got you strung out on drugs and booze?"

"Shut up! Quit trying to second guess me and listen. Since the day I talked to you on my patio I have done nothing but set up my life to find out who killed Eileen. Now I know who and why."

"Why? That's a good one. Why would he kill his own daughter."

"See? You weren't listening. Charles, his chauffeur, was Eileen's real father."

"The more you talk, Bob, the worse this gets, for you that is. Maybe I should do more than just evict you. Maybe I should have you committed, for your own safety."

"You get your ass down here and I'll show you documented proof, buddy. Tonight. You fly in tonight."

"I'm busy."

"Do you know how many people have died because of this mess? Five. This has got to stop. Henry has got to be stopped. Now whose side are you on, mine or his?"

I waited through a long pause.

"All right. But I want to see proof of every word you've said. Or, I swear, Bob, I'll have your ass carted off to the nearest mental ward."

After he hung up, I held the phone against my head for a moment. Lori's hand patted my shoulder.

"That wasn't much fun, huh?"

I took a deep breath and dialed another number. My jaw clamped as I waited through two rings.

"Hello?" Henry answered.

"I want to talk."

"Really. What about? My limousine? You do realize I will take the damages out of your allowance."

"I'm not paying you one fucking dime. I expect you to pack up your office at Ashland Steel and vacate, beat it, vamoose."

Long pause. "Why would I do that, Robert?"

"Because I own the controlling interest."

"You are babbling nonsense."

"Quit playing the goddamn games. We both know I have Eileen's original will. Not one of your doctored copies. The original."

"Then I suggest you contact an attorney."

"You better believe I'll do exactly what I have to. That means, I will be coming to my office tomorrow morning. Either you have my desk empty or I'll shit-can your stuff. There is not one thing you can do about it."

"You are so wrong, Robert. The police will simply escort you out of here. My attorney has already filed a contest to all other wills Eileen may have written. That original you have is worthless. And remember, I hire only the best legal minds. There is no one who can stand up to quality."

I decided to strike. "Really? Is that why you had Eileen killed?"

"You're insane!" He actually laughed. "Go see a good psychiatrist. I will even pay for that myself. I have a business to run. Good-by!"

Harry cocked his head at me. "By the looks of that shit-eating grin, you just ate a mouse."

"Not yet, but I'm getting the mouse closer to the bait."

"Now what?"

"It may get uglier. Are you two still with me?"

"Hey, I haven't had this much fun since . . . since . . . I can't remember when!"

"And I don't like repeating myself, Bob." Lori lifted one eyebrow, immediately reminding me of her emotional investment.

I nodded. "Well, like I told Henry, tomorrow morning I take over my office."

The guard at the gate of Ashland Steel refused to allow me entry. The first rays of the sun over the distant bluffs glinted gray off the black brim of the man's hat.

I turned to Donald in the Mustang's passenger seat. "What would you do to one of your employees who acted this rude?"

He sighed heavily. "Bob! Just go to the visitor's parking and wait for the place to open. This can be handled without a scene."

I threw my arm across the back of the seat and looked over my shoulder at Harry and Lori. "Should we do what my brother says or should we drive through the pansy-assed barricade?"

Harry thought a moment. "Did you get insurance on my car when you bought it?"

"Fully covered."

Together, Harry and Lori shouted "Go for it!"

I smiled at Donald. "Out voted!" My foot drove the accelerator to the floor. Tires squealed. The guard jumped back and the Mustang lurched forward. The wooden bar smacked the wind-shield, snapped, and disappeared over the roof of the car. A crack in the windshield slithered across Donald's side. He pushed himself back as if expecting the glass to strike him. Lori and Harry hooted. We sped across the empty lot toward the large brick building.

I saw the sign at Henry's reserved spot but couldn't stop before running over it. The car bounced on the concrete tire bumper, the pan scraping painfully. I slammed on the brakes a few feet from the front entrance, the tires skidding on the thick, green sod.

"You're acting like a goddamn teenager, Bob," Donald huffed. "There's guards at the door. Do they look like they're going to let us in?"

"I guess we'll just sit here and stare back at them. That should unnerve them a bit. At least until Henry arrives with the keys. That shouldn't take too long."

"Accompanied by the police, no doubt. You told me you would handle this peacefully. But, I should have known better. I'm getting out of this car so I can talk to Henry first. Maybe I can calm him down long enough to make some sense of this."

"Do whatever you have to, Donald. Harry, test the mike. Is everything on?"

Click. Whir. Click. "Yup. Working and ready. Word is the tape recorder is waiting," Harry spoke up from the back seat. "This stuff from Electronic City is some neat shit. Definitely better than guns, Bob."

Donald stared at me in disbelief. I grinned happily, then waved at the watching guards, beckoning them outside. As the minutes dragged by, the four men warily filed out the door. One man directed them into a semblance of a line in front of the doors. They didn't look professional or enthusiastic.

Just as the sun cleared the horizon, Lori settled down in her seat with "They're coming!"

The convoy drove by the guard shack without hesitating. The blinking red and blue lights of the police cars reflected off the long cream colored vehicle in the lead.

"Henry must've bought a new limo," Harry quipped.

"Why did he bring so many cops?"

I shrugged. "Witnesses?"

"You should become a comedian, Norris!" Harry wasn't laughing. "I'm not so sure about this."

"You just be sure the equipment keeps working."

"Yeah, yeah. The receiving end just clicked at me."

"Donald?" I called out. He had gotten out of the car. "Don't you blow this!"

Henry's limo stopped in front of his flattened sign. The cop cars fanned out behind him.

"And don't you do anything stupid! Give me a chance!" Donald ordered as he started forward.

As the three of us piled out of the Mustang, cop car doors flew open and men jumped out.

"Don't shoot! Nobody has guns!" Donald yelled frantically, running forward waving his arms. I was suddenly glad his draft number hadn't come up or he wouldn't be here now, looking like a scared fool.

Lori yawned and settled one hip against the car. "I hope this works. I can't function on a couple hours sleep."

I started to comment but swallowed my words as Henry and Sergeant Morten stepped from the limo. They walked right passed Donald.

Henry pointed at me. "Arrest this man for trespassing and destroying property."

Before Morten could even open his mouth, I responded, "You're not arresting anybody! I have legal proof that I own this business, Morten! I suggest you take this fairy fruitcake with you and get off my property."

Morten hesitated just long enough for me to turn to Henry. "I have a judge on his way here. Harry . . ." My thumb pointed to where Harry talked over a cell phone, ". . . is talking to him now. We can have a friendly little chat while we wait. What should we talk about? Oh, yeah. Why did you say you had Eileen killed?"

"You are totally out of your mind. Now, I want you out of here. You can talk to Winters. He has all the proof necessary to counter any of your asinine claims. Sergeant Morten has already seen the papers."

"Well, I'm sure your wimpy little attorney is hiding back in the limo, but this is really just between us . . . you and me. So why don't you call off your worthless watchdog here and we'll talk . . . while we wait."

Donald stood to the side, shifting from foot to foot, like a kid who has to go to the bathroom, but doesn't know how to interrupt and ask. I motioned for Lori. She took him by the arm and led him back to the Mustang.

Henry sighed sharply. "I have nothing to hide from Sergeant Morten. Do you remember I mentioned how I like to gamble, in a business sense? Well, the Sergeant and I have a bet. He says you will go to jail and rot there. I say you will drop these teenage antics and work for me, either at Ashland Steel or Bison Insurance."

"I guess you both lose. When I'm finished here, Henry, you won't have a business or a job, maybe not even a life." I looked at Harry. He clicked the phone closed and held up five fingers. "We have a few minutes before the judge arrives. Why not humor me with some answers, Henry?"

He glared at me a long minute. "I do believe Judge Snyder is on call today. We had drinks last night. Yes, he did tell me that. So, I'll be patient and play your game until he gets here. Of course, you know I will deny everything anyway and my word will carry so much more weight than yours. Why shouldn't you know the truth before you go away forever. Your wife meddled in my business and she was removed. Did I feel badly? Not particularly. Her mother proved to be a whore and the daughter an untrustworthy disgrace who regretfully carried my name."

"What a cold-blooded sonofabitch you are! Why didn't you have me killed, too?"

"You were never a threat, until recently. I realized you would actually figure everything out, and you had Eileen's will. I undermined your credibility and you graciously cooperated there. Now, if you don't continue to cooperate, Sergeant Morten will incarcerate you."

I laughed. "No, Henry. I'm done kissing your ass. The judge coming? It's not your piddling little Snyder, but a retired Federal judge. Remember, they are appointed for life? Anyway, Jerry Williams is an old friend, a neighbor, in fact. He's already seen the will in my possession. He's perfectly willing to look over the one Winters is clutching. I think Jerry can make an objective evaluation. I'll honor it, anyway. How about you? Do you have any honor left?"

Henry glanced at Morten then narrowed his eyes at me. "I thought you said you had called for the judge on duty."

"Did I? I don't think so. I just said 'a judge was coming.' Is your mind slipping, Henry? Maybe it's getting a little over-loaded with too much responsibility."

"Your sense of humor is lost on this audience, Robert. If this Jerry is indeed who you say and your neighbor, I'm sure he has observed your irrational behavior these past few weeks."

"As a matter of fact, we have talked . . . ah, like you and Snyder, over drinks. No, Henry. He will believe me."

"Words. Words prove nothing, Robert."

"Unless they are tape recorded. I have a mike on me and a very trust-worthy police officer in a van about a mile away. Oh, I didn't mention Judge Williams and the County Attorney are listening with him! Must have slipped my mind."

Henry's eyes widened in a true deer-in-the-headlights look. But the next moment he stepped close to Morten, his lips in a snarl, his voice pitched low. "You get your goddamn gun out and shoot this bastard, or you'll lose every penny you've ever gotten from my people!"

Morten's mouth opened and closed. He backed away from Henry like the man was contaminated. One, two pops sounded. Morten doubled over and fell to the ground. Henry turned and I looked down the narrow tunnel of his small gun. Smoke drifted from the opening, then I glimpsed a flash. A burning fist hit my chest and I fell back, not stopping until my head hit the ground. My hands dug at the holes in my silk shirt. Never liked pastel blue anyway.

A car door slammed beyond my head. I rolled over and raised up. The cream colored limo backed between cop cars, veered crazily, then tires squealed at it surged away.

Donald wrapped his arms around me and lifted me to my feet. He didn't let go as I tried to balance myself. His arms felt pretty good. Then Lori and Harry added their arms to the celebration.

"Bob, wow, man!" was all Harry could manage.

"You are crazy!" Donald muttered.

Lori kept repeating "Are you okay? Are you okay?"

I wiggled free from them, my hand rubbing over the heavy vest. "Do you think Roy will notice the cut now, Harry?"

"You sonofabitch!" Harry pounded me on the back. "The cops are coming towards us instead of chasing him."

I looked up and saw the uniformed officers cautiously walking forward. "Like hell! Get in the car!"

"Don't you think Roy's calling for assistance? That's their job."

"I'm not losing the bastard now!"

Donald backed away. I thought maybe he really had to go to the bathroom and left him there. Lori dove in the rear seat as I took the wheel and Harry slid into the passenger side. I noticed they snapped on their seat belts. As I gunned it and spun sod into the air, I glimpsed Lori putting on the headset and talking into the transmitter.

A uniformed officer tried to flag me down. I hit the horn and he jumped to the left. The entrance guard waved me on like some rookie cop directing traffic.

"Bob!" Lori yelled excitedly. "Roy says Henry's westbound on Maple. State Patrol has road blocks up. They should stop him in about five minutes.

I took a turn on two wheels. Harry's hand gripped the dash as his body stiffened, pressing him in the seat.

"Brake the goddamn car before you turn. You ain't even going in the right direction. This is south. Maple's north."

"He'll turn off Maple and head-to the Pink Horn. His luggage and passport are waiting, remember?"

"How do you know he'll do that?"

"Expressway entrance on Maple. Straight shot downtown. No lights. My gut tells me he doesn't intend to be caught."

"Well, you got lights!"

"I'm an expert now!"

"Shit!" Lori squeaked.

"Harry, reach under the seat for that stolen gun."

"I ain't reaching nowhere, not the way you're driving!"

"It rolled back here." Lori called. "I got it!"

I glanced in my rearview mirror and caught the flicker of red and blue lights. "Lori, did you tell Roy about the Pink Horn?"

"Yeah. He notified the State Patrol. The cars behind us are city police. They think you shot Morten. Roy's trying to talk to them now, but they don't believe him."

I ran a red light, barely missing a taxi. The Mustang banged over a pothole. I prayed a tire wouldn't blow. A block ahead I thought I saw a cream car. The traffic slowed. I swerved into the left lane, glad the oncoming traffic was at least two blocks away.

"Bob! Roy says the State Patrol is with us, but the city cops are siding with Henry. They're arguing jurisdiction, but the state boys have stopped the city from chasing us. We got a clear shot."

The car hit bottom on the dip of an intersection. Something rubbed and the steering tightened. Burnt rubber and smoke drifted into the car. I couldn't quite make the next turn and had to hit the sidewalk. A tire rolled passed, sparks shot up beside Lori's window, and the brakes locked. Harry leaned against the dash, swearing words I had never heard before. The motor raced on high, so I switched it off. The Mustang stopped on the curb, it's rear end blocking the sidewalk.

"Where the hell are we?" Harry yelled.

"Open your eyes and you'll see. Half a block from the club. Lori, give me that gun. You two stay here."

"Like hell we will," Lori said as she slapped the gun in my palm.

Harry almost fell out of the car, his expression pained. "Tell me you are gonna fix my car."

"Of course."

"Then I'll go with you and make sure you don't get yourself killed. Yo, look! The limo's pulling away."

"He isn't in it."

"How can you be so damn sure?" Harry demanded as we jogged toward the club.

"Street smarts!"

Harry flattened himself beside the door, crouched, then pushed it inward and slipped inside. I stepped through the opening, immediately moving to my right and dropping down as well. I could hear Lori behind me, her breath shallow and panting.

The entry was a curved series of steps, dark now with the only illumination coming from the mirror lights of the bar and scattered indirect lighting.

Harry tapped his chest, then pointed to a hallway beyond the bar. Lori's hand came over my shoulder, pointing to a frosted door on the other side of the room. She got Harry's attention and he nodded.

"That way," she whispered against my ear. "Did you pull the slide to put a round in the chamber?"

I did before turning slightly to push her onto her butt. "Stay. Don't let him out that door."

Her lips puckered in a pout. She folded her arms and nodded. She knew I was excluding her. I quickly kissed those lips then ran across the darkened, deserted dance floor.

The frosted door had a degree of suction. I finally opened it and slipped into the shadowed lighting and chlorine smell of a swimming pool. A Grecian-type pillar shielded me as I tried to assess what I faced. A dozen or so naked men lounged around the pool, too engrossed in one another to notice my intrusion. I caught a glimpse of Henry as he stepped into the sauna. After jamming the gun into my waistband, I briskly walked to the door.

Steam billowed into my face as I entered. I stumbled into the bench. Two fat men clung to one another on the top bench. They stared at me then turned their heads to look across and down. Orange flashed. The two men screamed. I ducked then launched myself at the shadow form, one thought driving me: Get my hands on his scrawny neck and choke the life from him.

My fingers grabbed his short, curly red hair, as he attempted to dodge me. The gun barked again. The fat men screamed again. I couldn't feel if I was hit, and didn't care as my arm snapped around his throat just like I had seen Lori do to Turner. The two pale-skinned polar bears bumped us in their panic to leave the small room. I backed out, Henry tight in my grasp. The gun fired into the ceiling twice more as he twisted.

Pool-side, I threw him onto the ceramic tile and stomped his gun hand. His scream echoed in the watery canyon. Picking him up by the hair with my left, my right punch created a familiar crunching sound. I let go. Like a fish, he flopped to the tile and slithered into the pool.

"Oh, no you don't," I muttered and jumped in beside him.

My feet didn't touch bottom. I opened my eyes and saw the his absurd slow-motion ballet as he sank. I kicked and shoved him out of the water, my hands on his throat. My fingers squeezed the narrow tube of flesh. Just as we started to sink again, he convulsed. His eyes glazed over before my face and I released him. I kicked away and let his body drift to the bottom.

At the pool's edge, I reached for a hold and felt a strong hand clasp mine. Harry stared at me one understanding moment then hauled me up. The wet vest weighted me down. Water ran off my clothes and puddled in my shoes. Harry shoved me onto a bench.

"Ambulance is on its way."

"He's down there, Harry."

"Lori just jumped in to drag him out. No one else watching had the balls."

"He had a gun."

"I remember. Are you sure you're okay?"

Lori broke the surface of the pool, gasping and sputtering. "Harry! Give me a hand." She lifted and splashed, pushing Henry in front of her.

Harry's mighty hand fisted his shirt collar and slid him onto the tile. Four men crept closer to gawk. Harry looked them up and down, his disgust obvious. "Okay, assholes. I don't need your help, but there is a lady present. Get some clothes on before the police get here!" They grabbed towels and ran for the door.

As if on cue, sirens sounded from just outside the building. Harry helped Lori from the pool. She shrugged at her wet clothes then pulled the blouse away from her curvaceous body. Her gazed settled on something and she started to bend down. Harry stopped her.

"The police need to find just Henry's prints on it."

She coughed and nodded.

I pushed up from the bench and stepped to Henry's side. His mouth hung open, his sightless eyes stared at the pool's reflections on the ceiling.

"Anyone know CPR?" I asked dully.

Harry looked all around. "Nope, guess not, Bob."

Guns drawn, police entered the pool then lowered their weapons and waved the paramedics in. Of course, their expert CPR was ineffective. Harry pointed out Henry's gun and one of the officers picked it up with a plastic bag.

Roy sauntered in, looked around the place and shivered. Some of the police agreed with his sentiments. He walked over and looked down at Henry as they covered him with a long beach towel. His hand pounded me on the back, half in congratulations, half in condolence. After glancing behind me, he stepped close and put one arm across my shoulder. Considering where we were, I frowned at him. He maintained his stance while they lifted the corpse onto a stretcher.

"Well, Bob, it's been a bad day and it's been a good day." His hand slid down my back and deftly pulled the gun from my waistband. Slipping it into his own waistband, he stepped away. One finger tapped the front of the vest. "You can just throw that thing away. It's been cut up, shot, and drowned. I think I'll have to replace it." He then cocked a finger at Harry. "You two watch over him. He hasn't quite got this street thing figured out."

Harry grinned back, but Lori bit her quivering lip.

"Hey, Roy!" Harry called out. "Think we could get a ride home. He wrecked my Mustang."

"Go find some clean . . . ah, unused towels, and I'll think about it," Roy said before going out the door.

I took a step, before Lori's hand on my arm stopped me.

"This may be bad timing, but I gotta ask. Now that the old fart's dead, and you've got . . . well everything, will this be a quick 'Thank you and good-by?'"

"What the hell are you talking about?"

"It's over. You don't need Harry and me any more."

"That's your opinion, not mine. Of course, like you said once, you and Harry have a choice. Mine is to see that Harry gets that new arm and a new car, not necessarily a red one, unless he wants it. And you can do whatever . . . well, whatever you want to dream. No more streets, no more threats. You can be safe."

"And respectable?"

"Definitely. In fact, I'll guarantee that."

"And what will Bob Norris be doing while I'm being respectable?"

"Let me think about that."

– THE END –